Da[rk] Horse

~ & ~

Other Stories

Dark Horse

~ & ~

Other Stories

DAVID ELLIS

atmosphere press

Author's Preface

Here are four stories. I hope that you enjoy reading them.

The common theme running through this collection might be 'journey' or, more specifically, 'journey into the unknown', odd things happening to ordinary people. In the first story, the traveller comes across a curious village while trying to escape a family emergency... definitely a journey in that one. The second story, 'Everywhere', sees our hero, Dougie, notice increasingly strange goings-on during a routine day at work. In 'The Devil in the Rainbow', young Aiden sets out on an adventure to follow some mysterious footprints, and in the final tale, Adrian and Blake battle it out for promotion at "Simkins"... and try to reconcile their differences at a very unusual pub.

'Soul Train' was written a while ago, around 1985 or thereabouts, while I was a student at Exeter University, the other tales are more recent. 'Soul Train' was inspired by Poe and the Sherlock stories of Conan Doyle, old fashioned, honest-to-goodness ghost stories. 'Everywhere' came out of a thought while on a bus, heading for work. Wouldn't it be strange if the person that sold you your morning newspaper looked the same as the driver of your bus who looked the same as the guy that welcomed you into your place of work?

'The Devil in the Rainbow', I confess, is a steal from an old folk tale that I first encountered as a boy. I used to love reading ghost and monster stories and constantly harassed my poor mother to buy books for me on these subjects. In one of these, I encountered a most perplexing case. On 9th February 1855, following a heavy overnight snowfall, God-fearing men and women awoke in villages scattered across South Devon in the south-west of England, to find new prints in their garden paths and surrounding streets and lanes. These marks, apparently made by a cloven hoof, similar to those of a donkey, extended for up to one hundred miles, crossing rivers and streams, traversing walls and, tantalisingly, appearing at both ends of drainpipes. Arranged in single file and seemingly branded into the snow, one obvious source of the prints was the Beast, the Devil himself. Surely this had been the night that Satan had visited Devon!

I have re-imagined this tale, telling the story from the perspective of the Sweet family, Aiden and his mother who live in the village of Flash on the edge of Dartmoor, ... and added a few extra twists.

In England, there are many public houses named after horses, the Black Horse, the Red Horse, etc. Recently, I had a thought about a pub that would be called the "Dark Horse", a phrase which of course has another meaning... in the "Dark Horse" you would certainly expect to find some unusual customers. By the way, there are pubs in all these stories, no better place to spin a yarn, so refresh your glass from the bar, gather round the fire, and I will begin.

Hope you enjoy the ride!

Table of Contents

The
Soul
Train

They say that age has a smell, I didn't used to believe it, no more than I expect you to believe me now, but my God, it's true I swear it. This smell of decay cannot be described, at least not by me, but once its evil fingers slowly start to grip you and the stench of things abandoned takes hold of your nerves, you'll not mistake it.

Such a smell held me in its grasp that dark, fearful night some ten years ago. Even now, at lonely times, the memories flood back, a wave of terror that floods my heart. Often, I have awoken from nightmares, dripping with sweat, every muscle in my cursed body as tight and tense as an iron bar, recently it has been getting worse, much worse, I feel that I must recount my experience to someone, anyone who might listen, and so, my friend, I am most grateful that you have decided to visit. Please sit down and make yourself comfortable. My story will take some time to tell.

The Gods were against me that night true enough, for why, I do not know, I had led a good life, happy, yet not with the indulgences that some require to achieve that state. I was married then, though I fear, not now. The effect on my sanity, the collapse that resulted from my experience, was too great for Sarah... my poor wife, to bear.

The twentieth of August , that was the date, in the year nineteen hundred and twenty-two, and it will be burned into my brain for all time. On the previous day, my darling Sarah's mother, an elderly, frail lady, had taken ill, and her loving daughter, understandably, had gone to be by her side. I had naturally wished to accompany my wife, but she had been reluctant to burden the old lady with any more visitors than was necessary. Regrettably, our worst fears were soon realised as, in due course, the dear soul passed away. Odd thing, sir, but on the very morning that she first took ill, the large mirror in our bedroom was discovered mysteriously cracked, a sure harbinger of ill-fortune, some might say.

With your forbearance, I shall continue my tale... So it was that I was alone in the house on that day, alone and miserable. On such occasions a man's mind may wander to find means of amusement. After pacing up and down our lounge for what seemed like many hours, though most likely was not, I concluded that a bracing drive in the country might be just the thing to boost my spirits.

This proved correct, initially at least. Thoughts of my predicament rapidly receded as I motored out of the village in which I then lived. You may know it, sir, Spellingham, a pleasant little hamlet on the edge of the South Downs. Our house was positioned most splendidly on the very edge of the village so that, in very short time, we could be amongst the open fields or walking in dark, secret woods. This fact had been largely responsible for my purchasing the property in the first place, but two months prior to the events which I am about to describe. Attempting to make the best of things, I considered that this drive would be an excellent opportunity for me to explore my new neighbourhood.

It was barely lunchtime when I left the house behind, and the sun was hot on my face, you may recall that we had a particularly hot summer that year, sir. The road that I decided to follow on that fateful day was one that I had not taken before. I realise that you may find the following comment foolish, but I have to tell you that I had not even been aware of its existence, being blind to this turning off the Brighton road before this extraordinary journey. What is even stranger is this; when, on later occasions, I questioned men in the village about my experiences, not one professed any knowledge of this road, even those that had lived in the locality for many years. What I do know, with utmost certainty, is that even if I ever find this road again (if this occurs, it will most surely be an accident on my part), I shall avoid it and urge all mortals to do the same. I am sure now sir, that road leads directly to the gates of Hell itself, as my narrative will confirm.

Hell was the farthest place from my mind on that day, and with good reason. The sky was blue, the leaves on the trees were green and full of life, birds sang joyfully from every branch, it was good to be alive. I was struck by the contrast with the predicament of my wife and her sick mother; truly, sir, life throws up such cruel conflicts. I will concede to you that my actions appear selfish, to appear joyful in the face of a family crisis, yet bear with me, justice will be seen to be done.

There were few people abroad on the road, an observation that I considered strange in view of the spectacular weather. In point of fact, sir, I saw no other living soul while driving on that road. I did not dwell on it at the time but have thought of it many times since, now realising that this was just one of many oddities and horrors that I witnessed on that day. I took a late lunch of sandwiches... prepared in the kitchen prior to my departure from the house... under the prettiest bridge that man has ever constructed. A stone-built beauty, it spanned a crystal clear river whose near-still waters reflected the trees that hung over it... words could not, and cannot describe the peace and beauty of that place. I was possessed of the feeling that I may have been the first human soul to observe it, that, until that moment, maybe it had not been witnessed by mortal man.

Sorry sir, are you cold? You appear to be shivering. I must agree that the temperature has dropped alarmingly in this room. I will feed the fire... ah, that is better already. A room is a sad place without a homely blaze, do you not think?

If you will allow, I shall return to my tale. I remained at the bridge for some time, or so it seemed. When I eventually made the decision to part from this fine place, however, my watch showed that only forty-five minutes had passed since my arrival. I returned to my vehicle and continued on my way, anticipating what other wonders lay ahead to discover. After driving across the bridge, the road passed rapidly into a great and thick wood. So high and dense was the canopy that no sunlight was able to penetrate, the way forward, therefore being very dark... as a consequence, I required all of my concentration to maintain progress. On several occasions, I narrowly missed running my car off the road into one of the many shadowy hollows that lined my route.

The forest proved unchanging and endless. I began to think that I should turn around and retrace my journey, being fearful of being overtaken by the true darkness of night. However, before I could effect this change of plan, the overpowering trees magically fell away. Suddenly and remarkably, I found myself driving up a street within a small village. Even today I find it hard to comprehend how this happened. It just transpired, without any warning or suggestion, that the undergrowth was thinning. Once out of the wood, however, it seemed that this village appeared to be a normal collection of houses interspersed with one or two shops, people going about their everyday business as one might do on such a fine day, I reduced my speed so as take in the sights. About a hundred yards on from my entry point, on the right-hand side, I noted a fine building, possibly the grandest of all that I had thus far seen. A sign, 'ROOMS', proud and bold, above the main entrance door caught my attention.

It was then that I made my most fateful decision, one that I shall regret for the remainder of my miserable existence.

I had a mind to stay overnight.

My thinking was principally guided by the lack of any pressing business at home, my dear wife not expected back for another few days. I parked the car in a small dusty clearing on the opposite side of the road and slightly further along, before turning back on myself to access the entrance to the hostelry, there being no obvious, more adjacent, parking place. A rather grand doorknocker cried out to be put into action, and shortly a pretty and engaging young girl opened the great, oak door. She was possibly eighteen years of age with the most dazzling blue eyes, sir, most notable. I reasoned that she may have been the daughter of the master of the premises, and this was confirmed in the short conversation that followed. Alice was her name, yes... Alice. She confirmed that rooms were available and indicated that I should follow her. I did so. The accommodation, just off a first-floor landing, was adequate, though I have to say that the grandeur of the exterior of the building was not reflected in the rather spartan nature of the interior. No matter, it was inexpensive, and as I was to be staying for but one evening, I judged that it would suffice. Once alone in my single room, sparsely furnished yet clean and in a good state of repair, a great tiredness overtook me, I should tell you, sir, that I was not a man used to driving for long distances. Now... well, my frail nerves will no longer permit me to drive at all.

Forgive me. I am digressing once again. I will return to my story.

I recall almost collapsing onto the small bed in a state of some exhaustion, grateful for the comforting softness beneath me. I then fell fast asleep. I have no knowledge of how long I did sleep that afternoon, for I had neglected to check my watch before my slumber had commenced. In any event, as I have previously indicated, the physical movement of the clock hand appeared to have little connection to one's impression of time's passage, just another curiosity of the adventure. One of the consequences of my experience that I now relate, sir, is an increasing obsession with the measurement of time. You may have noted my large collection of clocks in the house; some find this strange, even oppressive. I receive few visitors these days, however, so it matters little.

I was awoken from my deep and dreamless sleep by a loud knock at the door, its vehemence suggesting that my intended visitor had been attempting to arouse me for some time. I rose in some disarray, though feeling refreshed, and opened the door. The girl Alice was standing beyond, seemingly startled by my sudden and somewhat unkempt appearance. I apologised for my state, provoking a smile and an inquiry as to whether I wished to take dinner. This mention of food beat away the last echoes of exhaustion... you will remember that I had eaten merely a light lunch. Therefore, I accepted her kind offer with enthusiasm, retreated inside my room to tidy myself, then followed my guide downstairs through the entrance lobby into a side room, this proving to be the establishment's small dining room. There were but four tables, if I recall correctly, and a single other guest. This gentleman was of approximately your age, sir, with a ruddy face and a most prominent nose, all indicating a love of the intoxicating liquor. He nodded cordially as I entered but made no further attempt to communicate during our meal. Speaking of this, it was truly a superb feast, if not fit for a King, then at least adequate for a Prince, and all served by the girl. A vast joint of beef, dripping with promise, potatoes, and an array of vegetables of eye-watering attraction. To follow, cheeses galore and sweet things aplenty and throughout, wine of great character, the latter producing a yearning for some more of the same. Consequently, when the girl returned to collect my spent plate, I informed her that I was minded to explore the village, and whether she could recommend an establishment where a man might enjoy a further drink. She nodded and gave swift directions to the principal village inn. After having done so, she gave a start, as if someone unseen had pricked her with a pin.

'But, sir, there is no need to leave our house tonight. We can keep your glass full for as long as you wish.'

'That is most kind, but, as I say, I have a mind to explore. I mean no disrespect to your hospitality.'

At this, she looked at me in an oddly distant fashion and made haste to leave the room. Her beauty was quite overwhelming, my friend, even frightening in some indefinable way, I have to tell you that I was struggling to reject dishonourable thoughts in that direction. Nevertheless, and with much reluctance, I left her company and that of my fellow guest and returned to my room. The shadows were lengthening as I looked out of my window, the sun sinking lower in the western sky. I had an unrivalled view of our great orb falling slowly toward the horizon as I lay on my bed. I watched, mesmerised as the colour of the sky changed from yellow through orange to red, with all intermediate shades being represented. Finally, the heavens began to darken as the bright life of day surrendered to the velvet blackness of night. Have you ever watched the sun set, sir? Ah... up until that time, neither had I, that evening was a revelation to me, I was stunned that nature was capable of generating so many hues. As the horrors of the night drew closer, I could not have been more content. How foolish I was, sir, how foolish. Yet, in my defence, I am sure that you will agree with me that the future is a closed book to all but witches and sorcerers.

Following the sunset, with the country well and truly in

the grip of old night, I decided to search out the inn of which the girl had earlier spoken. I washed and left my room, still feeling at peace with the world. Once downstairs, I saw her again. I recall thinking that it was somewhat strange that a girl as callow as this should seemingly have responsibility for the running of the entire establishment. I had not seen any other individual in authority, no mother or father or other member of staff. I was very taken with her, as I may have mentioned, and, forgiving any immodesty on my part, sir, I believed that she was attracted to me in some measure. The glance that she had directed at me at the foot of the stairs as she prepared to show me to my room would have been familiar to all who have been loved by another. In that moment, thoughts of my own courtship stormed my mind, initiating, I should admit, a sensation of guilt.

Her eyes caught mine as we passed one another in the lobby. I smiled, choosing to say nothing, opening the door of the house and stepping into the night. I stood for a time to allow my eyes to become accustomed to the low light levels, noting that the road was empty of humanity... no-one was abroad. Lifting my head to the heavens, I observed no moon, but the skies were a riot of stars, no wind disturbing the preternaturally still air. I had no heavy coat with me, merely a light jacket, a consequence of my lack of forward planning, but such protection was unnecessary on this warm evening. Around me, the starlight partially illuminated the buildings of the village, lights burning from some windows helping to inject some homely cheer into the scene. I turned to walk up the street, enjoying the peace of this summer night. I passed a store and some stables before the object of my quest became visible.

The Inn

This appeared a substantial pile, but in the dimness, it was difficult to draw further conclusions concerning the nature of the place. Some unknown influence caused me to move with more urgency than before. I entered the building quickly, without the normal apprehension that might accompany such an action in an unfamiliar place. Inside, I was pleased to discover that the snug was small and agreeably intimate, oak beams supporting a low roof. Scattered around the space were tables, equipped with rough-looking chairs, again made from oak. Light was provided by a number of cheery lamps introducing a cosy brightness to the room. Custom was fair, several groups of men sitting around the great tables talking and drinking, discussing those topics that you and I have chewed over a thousand times, though in your case, sir, I would presume in establishments of possibly higher standing.

I would imagine that you are expecting me to report that all heads turned toward me as I entered, and that conversation stopped. No such thing, sir, no-one so much as glanced at me. Pausing momentarily to appraise my surroundings further, I migrated to the bar, and there I discovered the most extraordinary innkeeper that one could possibly imagine.

To suggest this gentleman was large is an understatement as vast as the man himself, a towering brute who loomed over me in a most intimidating fashion. His face was one I shall remember until the end of my time. I should maybe qualify that remark for one could not 'see' very much of the face at all, much of it being concealed behind a monstrous beard. The eyes were open to the air, though, and these were wild indeed, but also cunning, seeming to probe your very soul, surgically intense they were. Such was the impact of this monster's appearance that I stood like a simpleton as he waited on my order... eventually, I came to my senses and requested the house ale. He served without a word. I well remember how agile his movements were, despite his bulk, the incongruity adding to the sense of the bizarre. After taking my money, he disappeared into the shadows at the far end of the counter.

I sat at a vacant table and took a welcoming draught of ale (ale seeming more appropriate in such a house than wine). Almost immediately, several of the men who had been wrapped in their own affairs up to this time approached me, creating initial concern on my part... the men were rough-looking types, and we have all heard stories of lonely travellers being set upon in such places. Such dishonourables would think nothing of cutting your throat and making off with any valuables that they could recover. I should not have been so fearful, for these individuals were smiling, and I quickly realised that they wished only to talk. Talk they did, and well into the night, all proving surprisingly articulate and know-ledgeable on current world events. They appeared genuinely interested in myself, asking where I had come from, the nature of my business and my destination, and many other matters. In return, they told me about themselves, they identified as local farmworkers and had been for all their lives. You have probably already started to question how such simple country folk could possess such intelligence on matters of high politics, business and diplomacy? I agree, but at the time, I did not ask this question of myself.

As we talked, we also drank, and the ale began to flow more freely than it should have done. Let me tell you this, sir, and this fact is worthy of note. I confess to having had rather a lot to drink on that night, but at no point did I become intoxicated, remaining alert throughout the horrors to come. God knows, had I had senses more effectively dulled by drink, I may have been more protected against the hell that was to follow.

As we drank, one of my companions mentioned that, on the previous day, he had taken five minutes more to eat his lunch than was permitted by the farm manager. He proclaimed this with great pride, and his fellows appeared suitably impressed. Then, as men do, each began to yarn stories of their own bravery in an effort to outdo the one before. Tales became more extraordinary and almost certainly less truthful in subject, some so ridiculous that I laughed aloud despite myself. The men did not demure and continued with accounts of pig wrestling and spending nights alone in the local graveyard. To my eternal regret, I became increasingly embroiled in the dares. I took advantage of a rare lull in the conversation to formulate my own contribution. The spirit of the night and the ale had gotten to my common sense and contaminated it with fool's courage.

The words that I used are as clear to me now as they were then.

'I swear by my mother's grave that I will take up any challenge, presented by any man in this room, irrespective of the danger that is involved.'

At this, silence descended on the inn, eerie in its totality. Other customers, who, until that time had been heartily engaged in their own conversations, suddenly looked up with expressions of interest on their faces. I was somewhat taken aback at this sudden reaction and sat back sheepishly, all eyes in the room, now on me. The silence continued to be almost tangible, all jocularity of the place submerged in the new mood. I became painfully aware of the enormity of my statement, but I am a gentleman, sir, and for me, there was no turning back.

Then, a voice as of a lost soul.

'I have a challenge.'

I turned to discover the source of the sound. It came from a man of whom I had not previously been aware, he was standing close to the door. I had the impression that he had just entered, yet, despite the silence of the previous minutes, I had heard no door open. No sound of entry. It was as if he had simply 'appeared'. All faces turned likewise to face the newcomer, and as he came forward into the light, a terror, so deep and dark, so ancient, ripped into my soul, suddenly the room was cold, icily cold. Grown men began to shiver, and those close to him withdrew as he advanced. A smell pervaded the room, a musty odour, a scent of death and cold graves and decay. No mortal should endure such dread as I endured, sir. Multiply the horrors from your worst nightmare by a thousand, and still you could not come close to the feelings of that night and of that place.

Despite my fear, I attempted to take in the details of the stranger. He was tall, unnaturally tall, and clothed in a great cloak, from neck to foot, despite mild weather. However, I knew that the sacred warmth of earthly realm could never penetrate the heart of such wickedness as that man conveyed. He walked with a strange, shuffling gait, such as a child when first learning. This man (and I use that word reluctantly, sir) approached me, seemingly ignoring the other customers, and the wall of dread, which I thought to be the ultimate that man could endure, grew tenfold more intense. As he came closer, I became more conscious of his phenomenal height, and of the foul stench that surrounded him. I also now observed that much of his face was concealed by the cloak, yet the eyes were visible.

They were red, sir... ah hah, I see by your expression that you do not believe me. Understand this; compared with events that I am yet to reveal, red eyes will appear the model of normality! Oh yes, two red eyes stared out at me... I was right glad of the presence of the cloak, for I could barely imagine what hideous features may have lurked beneath it. Fangs, maybe, pointed ears... cloven hooves instead of feet? Only one being could possibly strike such terror into God-fearing men. I was convinced then, and I am convinced now, that that thing that stood before us on that night was the Devil himself, the Beast of all our nightmares. I imagine that you begin to doubt my sanity, sir, you may well be correct in your diagnosis, but will you give a sick man the opportunity of completing his tale, even if it is solely out of pity? I am most grateful. Should you like another drink of whisky? I confess I take too much these days, but it does wonders in easing my passage through the turbulent nights. No? Please forgive me while I pour myself a dram. You see that the memories are causing my hand to tremor.

The creature spoke again, the voice disconcertingly normal now, and of a gentleman, rather like your own, sir.

'I have a challenge to tempt the bravest of men and the most foolish, the two qualities being equivalent'... following the words, he gave a little laugh, as if amused by his own witticism. Terror froze my lips as he continued.

'That is, if you are still interested?' This comment was definitely aimed at myself.

I could not speak. His... its, I do not know what description to use, eyes closed slightly, and I knew what foul mouth he possessed was smiling beneath its dark cover. He clearly interpreted my silence as approval, and so continued.

'Excellent, in a short while, a train will pass by the station in this village, as it does on this day every year.'

Instantly, the customers, who, until this time had been as mute as myself, registered recognition. They looked at one another knowingly, some nodding their heads as if now, they appreciated the awful truth. The inn was filled with a low murmur.

'It is said that the passengers on this train are the souls of mortal men and women on their final journey to Hell.' The last word echoed round the room, 'Hell... Hell... Hell,' until my head was full of its evil.

'It is also said that the mere sight of this train is enough to strike a human dead, is that not so?'

The thing swung round with remarkable speed, to look at the gathered clientele, they unconsciously drew back... again the horror uttered a slight laugh, utterly humourless, proud of his power to terrify the innocent. He then turned back to me.

'Just foolish superstition though, sir, I am sure you will agree. Tall tales told by old women on dark nights like these, to strike fear into young ones, not for educated gentlemen such as yourself.' His eyes smiled again.

'My challenge is this, sir, that you agree to walk to the station on this night and merely watch as the train passes through... but then...,' he added dramatically, 'There will be no train... will there?'

He paused once again.

'The reward for carrying out this trifling mission will be the acquisition of all of the material possessions for which you have always longed.'

I did not request details of how this stranger could fulfil his promise... following my assessment of his true identity, I did not doubt that he could fulfil his side of the bargain... also, fear maintained its tight grip on my tongue.

Following a brief pause, I croaked out a response, my voice hardly audible.

'And if I refuse to accept your challenge? What will happen?'

'Nothing,' he replied. 'But those treasures will remain where they currently lay.'

I think that I knew, sir, where those treasures of which he spoke, had their nest. Following his challenge, he moved clumsily toward the door. Once there, he turned again and bored into me with those cruel eyes.

'Remember, all you have ever wanted!'

Then he was gone.

The instant after the door closed, I rose and raced toward it. Sir, I was there but seconds after the fiend left, yet, on opening that door and looking out into the night, I saw nothing, and there was no sound of receding footsteps to betray its presence. The monster had vanished, returned to that infernal place from which it had come, knowing that the seed of greed had been sowed into my cursed mind. So it was, on that damned night, I made the decision which was to destroy my life. On returning inside, all saw from my face what I had witnessed, or more accurately, not witnessed. God bless them, they attempted to deflect me from responding to the challenge.

'Do not do it!' An old man shouted. 'The Evil One will have you in his power, and there will be no escape.'

'Take it from us, sir, we have all lived hereabouts for all of our lives, and we know that this train is to be feared. None of us will venture abroad to the station on this night. Why do you think we are all here, now, in this inn? To give us courage, sir, that is why, to be together on this night. All of our womenfolk are safely in their beds. You will find no-one on the street.'

God, God! Why did I not listen to my potential saviour, and to the other saintly men who tried so hard to save me... but I thought only of reward, the Devil's gold, of jewels and property.

'Do not fear for me,' I remarked. To my amazement, there was a certain element of jollity in my reply. 'Surely you well-educated gentlemen cannot believe in this... foolish legend, this story?' I looked around at my colleagues, many of them turning their faces away, refusing to meet my gaze. Did I believe that the train would arrive? Maybe, I cannot be certain what I did or did not believe. If the story were to be true, maybe I had some hope that I could defy the Evil One, that I could witness this train to Hell and live to tell the tale. I just do not know, sir. I suspect the promise of riches beyond my imagination had corrupted my brain, my own avarice overcoming the powers of reason. I made ready to leave. The vacant expressions on the faces of my companions will haunt me to my grave. They clearly believed that I would not return.

I moved slowly across the bar in a supernatural silence. Not a word or any other sound could be heard. Even my shoes appeared to make no noise on contact with the stone floor. On reaching the door, I turned to say my farewells, and my voice sounded as an explosion in the deathly quiet. I turned back to open the old door, issuing forth a barely audible creak. As I did so, a voice spoke out from behind.

'You are a fool, sir!'

I whirled around quickly, my senses on edge, but all faces were the same, silent, shocked, paralysed by a mortal fear of the unknown, and fearful for me. I considered asking who had delivered the insult, but decided against it. This was not the time for such distractions. I, therefore, said nothing, closing the door behind me after stepping into the night. The stars had gone, having retreated behind a thickening yet invisible cloud. The light emerging from the houses was no longer sufficient to provide the required illumination, darkness had won its battle. The domestic glow from the windows had lost its cheeriness, all was now cold and soulless, inhuman.

Not having encountered the station *en route* to the inn, I reasoned that it must lay further along the principal road. The blackness was such that I had to almost feel my way forward by clinging to hedges and fences as I progressed, almost falling on several occasions, just righting myself in time. The preternatural quiet appeared to follow me as I inched my way forward, almost a physical entity in itself. Sir, I cannot describe my emotions as I made my slow way onwards. No adequate words are available to me. I ask that you use your imagination to replace the poverty of my description.

Following some indeterminate period, I reached the end of a row of buildings, still having passed nothing that had resembled a railway station. Surely, even in this almost total darkness, I would not miss the crucial destination? Then... I noticed, coming into view ahead, another shadowy structure looming out of the murk. Could this be it? From this distance (whatever that was, it was impossible to say), it seemed too large to be a house or outbuilding. I cannot emphasise enough just how poor was the light... I strained and squinted my eyes to capture every possible ray, the building ahead distinguishable only by a slight discontinuity in shading from the surrounding air. I walked tortuously toward it, breathing heavily, not from any physical effort, but purely through anxiety, several times stumbling though never catastrophically. Even had I fallen, I suspect that I would have experienced no pain, all my sensory machinery directed toward the need of the moment. Sweat broke out on my forehead and in the palms of my hands as I neared my target, heart racing dangerously and every muscle as taut as iron.

Suddenly I was there, and it was indeed the station, a low-slung, unprepossessing building, the purpose of the place being quite literally signalled by the presence of a semaphore signal pylon, rising above what must have been the tracks, just to the right of the structure itself. Whilst leaning against a convenient wall in order to catch my breath, I noted my disarray. My jacket was torn in several places after contact with unseen thorny hedges, and my hair was dishevelled through constant wiping of a sweaty forehead. Having arrived, I was immediately filled with a grim determination, yet one major obstacle now confronted me... being night-time, of course, the building was securely locked, I had failed to even consider this eventuality in my earlier addled state. A large iron gate barred my path, and I rattled it pointlessly. Yet the Devil was not to be confounded, a man suddenly appearing from behind the gate. Understand me, sir... when I say 'appeared', that is exactly my meaning. One moment not there, the next, there. I discerned no detail concerning the fellow, but could hear the jangling of keys and shortly, the gate opened noiselessly. Without a further thought, I stepped inside.

'Follow me', said he and led the way forward, around the front of the deserted station building and down a side passage. Mysteriously as we progressed, the air appeared to become gradually lighter, so that by the time we arrived on the platform, all was relatively well-lit. There were no lamps or other source of this ethereal glow, but this somehow seemed a minor peculiarity, just one more in this cabinet of curiosities.

The light allowed me to see that I was accompanied by a short, rather stout man dressed in the unmistakeable uniform of station-master. He appeared very old, face riven by deep wrinkles, and every movement was slow, seemingly painful, indicative of bad joints, I suspected. A pair of tiny, nervous eyes darted here and there, possibly in expectation of some undesirable event. I looked down at his hands, they were gnarled, twisted, almost claw-like, and they opened and closed continuously like pincers. This was a frightened man, yet his voice was steady, rich, and resonant, a most striking feature. I tried to make conversation.

'Is there a train due tonight?' I asked inadequately. He gave a little laugh. Where had I heard that laugh before? He turned the corner of his mouth upwards in a rather curious way.

'Well, we do expect a train of sorts,' the booming voice echoed around the place alarmingly, suddenly there were many station-masters. 'That is, there is one expected...' he looked straight at me, and for once, the jerking eyes were still, 'But no-one'll be wanting to catch it!' He looked around at the empty platform, seemingly using the lack of any waiting passengers to emphasise his hypothesis.

'I do not wish to catch it, merely to observe it,' I shuddered at the consequences of the former.

'Can't do one without the other,' shot he back, accompanied by another laugh. With that, the station-master, if that he be, walked off toward the station building, leaving myself on the platform.

'No, wait,' I cried, wishing not to be left alone in such a God-forsaken place. Even the company of this strange Charon-like character was better than nothing, but my entreaty was to no avail.

'What for?' Came the laughing response, and he was gone. I was very much alone.

Now sir, if I could have had ten minutes more on that platform. I may yet have saved myself. I could perhaps have talked myself around, and good sense could have prevailed, and I may have rejected the ridiculous challenge at this critical moment.

But I had no such time, for no sooner had my attendant left than I heard it.

Far away it was, at first, far away in space and time, yet to break through into the earthly dimension from the other place. In the beginning was the sound, a mere murmuring, but louder it grew until it became the unmistakeable roar of a raging locomotive, crashing and snarling as its infernal driver sought to wrench every last grain of power. I hear now the clanking of the carriages as they followed their master, wheels screaming over tracks subdued by such extreme speed. I was numb, frozen to the spot as the dreadful realisation hit home. 'Oh, yes, the train will be running tonight, my friend, who said that the train will not be running this night? Does it not always run on this night?'

Slowly my body began to shake, first my legs, and then the affliction spread like a wave to my arms and hands. I was bathed in sweat, my hands shining like gold in the strange artificial light. I wanted to move so desperately but could not. I was not even able to turn my head to observe what was coming down the track... but I heard it. Oh God, I heard it, sir! Louder and louder, the snarling engine, the screaming carriages, faster and ever faster, now completely in our world.

A horror that can travel through any existence, in any form to collect that which is required by that Apostate. This was truly the Soul Train, which needs no fire or coal, a train that travels on the evil in our souls, and that is a track without end, sir.

It was close now, so very close, soon it would pass, as would my life, surely.

Then I caught the single, glaring light at the heart of the engine, a monstrous yellow eye that could see all, and then... it roared past. Thanks be to God that its speed was such that no detail could be perceived. Merely a raging blur of metal and glass that was gone in a second, and following its disappearance, a gradual diminuendo of sound, as it receded into the distance, back to the Dark Place from which it had come, the night now silent again, silent and still. I was slowly released from my paralysis, first, my head agreed to move, and then I could flex my arms, and even walk unsteadily. Suddenly there was a scream, and the howl came from my own lips. A long and terrible sound, that of a wounded creature close to death.

I am nearly at the end of my tale, sir, though not of my nightmare. I ran away from the station like a banshee, somehow found my car, and drove home that very night, leaving my belongings at the hotel and arriving home in the early hours of the next morning. Once back at the house, I parked the car and was immediately overcome with exhaustion, pure adrenalin having sustained me over the previous twelve hours. Taking to my bed, I slept for four hours, but I regret to say, my relief was but temporary. As I regained consciousness following my sojourn, the full horrors of my experience returned to my mind... would this torment never end?

I adjourned to our small bathroom... astonishingly, sir, it occurred to me, in the midst of my despair, that I had not shaved for two days! A shave would at least occupy me for a short while and might begin to impose a sense of normality on a situation that was far from normal. I stood before the sink, above which was hung a small mirror... I suspect you have something similar, sir.

I looked into the mirror.

What do you think I saw looking back at me, sir, on that morning? Why it is a foolish question, obviously... what does a man see in a mirror... surely the same man that looks into it?

No sir!

No face stared back at me on that morning, the mirror containing no image of me or of any human. So, it had come to pass. I had now to accept, a being that presents no reflection in a mirror, is no being at all, merely a ghost, a wraith, with no substance... and no soul, sir!

From that day forward, my life was slowly torn apart, destined, in due course, to lose my wife, my house, and my business. This place, rented for a modest sum, is my home now. Sir, I see that you are sceptical, your expression reveals your mood in a most remarkable way. Let me read your mind, you are thinking that I am alive, seemingly in good health. I appear to have survived the visit from Hell, soul or no soul. I agree. I felt similarly after I had calmed down. Indeed, my mood lifted over the next few days, and the awful events withdrew themselves from the forefront of my mind. Soon, my darling wife returned, her mother's condition had stabilised, a short and cruel delay in what was to come. Things for the moment were looking more promising.

And then... forgive my voice, sir. It tends to shake every time I recount this final chapter. The occasion in question was the first in which my wife and I were together in our bedroom since my adventure, this being the day on which she had returned from her mother's. Try to imagine the scene. I was standing in front of the full-length mirror as I prepared for bed. I should add that the circumstances, even of this everyday event were curious, however. The mirror of which I speak had been delivered only that day, replacing one which had been broken; you may recall this incident from the early part of my narrative. My encounter with the bathroom mirror from some days previously was far from my mind, though I must say that, at our meeting earlier in the day, my wife had commented negatively on my new beard... unsurprisingly I had ceased to shave... and so I should have been reminded.

Therefore, sir, this occasion was to be the first time since the terror that my wife was able to, or I should say, should have been able to, see myself in a mirror.

Sarah, my wife, was sitting on the bed at the critical moment, and as she turned toward me, she uttered a most piercing scream. I was mortified and feared that she had taken ill. I implored her to tell me what was wrong. She was staring at me, through me, at something behind. Instinctively I whirled around to look at the mirror, and my heart stopped. All the old fear came back, multiplied by a thousand, sir.

I looked into the mirror and saw the room reflected into my eyes.

But not myself, sir.

Of course, there was no reflection of myself in the mirror.

What could I say? I had said nothing to Sarah on the subject of my hideous excursion. As I attempted to calm her with false, soothing words, we held each other tight, yet, as I have already mentioned, she was unable to deal with the awful truth and left shortly afterwards.

My tale is complete, sir. The demon-train has taken my soul. Where may it be now, on the track to some infernal place, or perhaps already arrived?

The gentleman that is now conversing with you, who is seated before you, sir, is a gentleman without soul. A gentleman who is, in essence, a ghost, trapped in this world with no hope of progression to a higher plane. Sir, this house is my Purgatory, and for me... there shall be no Paradise.

Everywhere

Dougie didn't normally dream; that's what made this one stand out. Looked at the bedside clock with the glowing red LED numbers as soon as he was conscious enough to recognise them, 07.00, it said. Rapidly noting that Laura had already gone downstairs, Dougie reflected on his dream. It had begun with himself, Dougie, the central character in the dream walking along a road in the middle of what appeared to be a desert, or some similar landscape, wasn't entirely clear to Dougie, and he thought worth noting in his review, that he had definitely experienced the dream as and from himself, he was the camera and the microphone, as it were, no independent commentary. Road was dusty and it may have been hot, Dougie wasn't quite sure... and that was one of the surprising aspects of the dream (apart from the biggie that Dougie didn't dream)... some parts of it were very clear with his 07.00 hindsight, and some weren't. Dusty road obvious, what lay either side, not so. Certainly, he was alone on the road, leastways at the start of the dream, though he kind of somehow knew that Laura wasn't too far away. In the dream, Dougie glanced down at himself, discovered that he was wearing a rather rustic brown jacket, similarly fashioned, unfashionable trousers, and unpolished brown boots, very

29

much not his normal style of attire. His immediate surroundings did not interest Dougie in his dream, so he paid little attention. From outside of his dream, he (Dougie) would have preferred him (Dougie) to show a little more interest, but it was obviously too late now that he had woken up.

In the dream, Dougie had just kept on walking alone for a while, and then, in the distance, a figure had appeared. Despite not being concerned with his environment, he couldn't miss this. It was right in front of him, right in his eye-line as he strode on. Figure got bigger as the two squeezed the distance that separated them. Now, more detail accompanied the higher resolution. Definitely male, medium-sized male, long cloak or cape, like a superhero or supervillain, Darth Vader maybe or a wizard, something on the head, wide-brimmed hat. Close enough to distinguish the face now, not yet close enough to discern detail, but that would come in the next minute.

'Hello!'

Christ, the chap was hailing him!

'Hello!'

'Hello,' replied Dougie, in the dream.

'Where are you headed?'

'Er, not too sure.'

'Well, you're heading in the right direction; sure enough you are.'

Voice was loud and confident, no discernible accent, would have gone down well on the BBC in the days of Lord Reith.

Bodies were a body's length apart now, near enough for Dougie to assess the face, smiley face, beaming smile, but the lips were tightly closed so no teeth visible, grey eyes, unexceptional, ruddy, lived-in skin, if he were a snake, it might be shedding time.

'Just you keep on going, friend. You'll get there in the end.'

Friendly stranger, flicked the corner of the hat and

sauntered past... then turned round from a distance of fifteen feet or so.

'Might meet some other folk on the way. My advice to you is to be polite and wish them well.'

Figure shrunk, inevitably as it continued its journey, hadn't fully disappeared by the time that Dougie woke up.

Get-out-of-bed time, no point in daydreaming about a night-dream. Wouldn't mention the dream to Laura... just one of those things, probably wouldn't happen again.

'We're out of "Shredded Wheat".'

'Sorry?'

'I said, we're out of "Shredded Wheat".'

'Oh.'

'Are you shopping today?'

'Don't I always shop on Tuesday?'

'Only asking!'

Dougie Wipton had to make do with just toast for breakfast, not a good start to the day, starting the day without cereal. How could they have run out of cereal? All you had to do was to check the box on a regular basis and purchase a new one when the little wheaty treasures were running on the low side.

'How come we have run out?'

'Don't ask me; you're the only one that eats the foul stuff.'

Dougie was accustomed to having these inter-room shouting conversations with Laura in the mornings, but he still found the experience tiresome.

'Can't you come through? I don't like shouting through walls!'

'I'm busy.'

How could she be busy? What was she doing?

'What are you doing?'

The reply was unintelligible, sounded as if she was speaking from inside a cupboard.

'What?'

'I said, I was sorting out our holiday things.'

'Why are you doing that now? I mean, we aren't going until the weekend... and it's only Weston!'

Silence, then a sound of footsteps.

Laura appeared at the door of the kitchen, 'I don't like talking through walls.'

'That's what I said.'

'Then we're agreed!' She smiled, and he smiled back.

'More doom and gloom on the wireless, I don't know why you listen to that radio four programme, it's so depressing, wars and strikes, always the same.'

'I don't think wars and strikes are quite the same, darling. People die in wars, not in strikes.'

'They do if doctors go on strike.'

'Doctors don't go on strike. They aren't allowed.'

She was tall, six-foot.

'Anyway,' he added, 'I like to keep abreast of the news.'

He was small, five-foot and a bit.

She was dark-haired.

'We should have something cheerful on, music.'

He was ginger, but sparingly so, balding early just like his dad, and not interested in pursuing the conversation. For him, the 'Today' programme was sacrosanct.

He was also looking at his watch... 'I'll be late for work.'

'Whose fault is that?'

He had a substantial beard, made him look rather gnomish.

'Will you get some more cereal?'

She gave him a kiss to force him on his way. He put on his jacket, looked like leather but wasn't. Dougie headed toward the exit, 'Don't forget, you know how much I like my cereal, only way to start the day.'

'You'll be late for work.'

'I know.'

As he walked down the garden path, Dougie noted that the apple tree had done its work. "Discovery", the very name had appealed. Gorgeous red fruit adorned the branches... ripe for picking. Must have been apples for days, but he hadn't noticed, unusual for Dougie... he noticed everything. How could he have missed ripe, red apples?

Decent garden, not too big but maybe larger than the house deserved. Not only did it contain trees (not too many, apart from the apple tree, there was also a Japanese maple, a flowering dogwood, and a crab apple... and various bushes that Dougie had planted... fancied himself as a gardener, did Dougie). A stream flowed along the edge of the plot, the water from which would eventually find its way, *via* various tributaries, to the River Eden.

Contentment was not a state that came easily to Dougie Wipton... traumatising over the breakfast-time lack of "Shredded Wheat", or the failure to spot ripening apples were par for the course; being late for work would add to the angst. In point of fact, he couldn't really be "late for work", because he could bloody well come and go as he pleased... up to a point... despite that he was more than capable of getting anxious about it. The reality was, he was AN IMPORTANT EMPLOYEE of a small software-design company and bloody good at software design. To say that he had the business over a barrel was a slight exaggeration, but Dougie knew that "they" would not want to lose him. For all his many faults, he was in possession of a sense of his own worth... in an understated sort of way.

Dougie had never been a driver, never fancied it, too

impatient, and so, every working morning, he enacted a ritual, began by walking to the bus stop at the bottom of the road. He was in possession of a bicycle and, on occasion, made use of it, those occasions often being associated with exceptionally good weather. This was not one of those occasions. It was not raining, but was as close to raining as not raining could be. Sky was full of wet, bound to come soon; it was just marking its time, determined to do the most damage, waiting for its chance. It might have been late August, but the weather marked not the seasons, not in fair old Blighty. No matter, Dougie would soon be on the bus, and after that, the rain could do its worst. He kept an umbrella at work which could be brought into service, if required, for the journey home.

He arrived at the bottom of the road, at the bus stop, his bus stop.

Glancing at his watch... who wears a watch nowadays, especially a software designer? Don't they all look at the time on their phones? Dougie still wore a watch, it had been his father's, and now it was his, expensive-looking timepiece, family heirloom. On looking at the family watch, Dougie realised that he was slightly early... most unlike him to be early at the stop. Must have walked slightly more quickly than normal. Definitely hadn't left the house any earlier.

Now he would have to wait, but only for a couple of minutes. What to do?

Dougie got his phone out, checked... stuff, e-mails, nothing too exciting there, bus would be here soon.

He strolled a few steps beyond the bus stop, and then back again, swallowing up a few minutes, then the bus appeared. A large grin broke out on Dougie's face. Good job, it was on time, more or less, maybe a minute-and-a-half late.

Dougie owned a "Ridercard", got him free travel on the local buses, though it wasn't "free", of course, since one had to buy the "Ridercard" in the first place. Nevertheless, it was cheaper than paying as you went... and the drivers didn't give change so unless you had the right money you lost out. Dougie had been stung by that one before, that's why he decided to buy the "Ridercard", well, that was one of the reasons.

The bus pulled into the stop, number forty-five. It was one of those new "hybrid" buses, reduced emissions, that sort of thing... and they were dead quiet. About a week ago, while waiting at the bus stop, Dougie had been distracted by an incoming e-mail to his phone, and while peering at the tiny screen, had quite missed the arrival of the number forty-five. It had ghosted by, totally unaware of his requirement to board. Dougie had blamed himself and had had to wait for the next one, twenty minutes in the future... he had needed to occupy himself for twenty minutes, now that had been a challenge!

No such problem on this occasion, Dougie brandishing his "Ridercard" at the driver upon boarding.

Strange.

Dougie had been catching this bus for... well, how long had he been at "Digital Solutions"? He knew exactly... three years, three years since he had first walked through those doors, and that was almost exactly one year after he had married Laura!

What was strange was the driver; he wasn't the usual driver. Over the years, Dougie had gotten used to seeing the same face, never knew the chap's name, naturally, but there had been some meeting of minds, a friendly 'mornin,' or 'have a good weekend,' or some other false "bonhomie". The regular driver had been a big fellow, lots of beard and sweat, always seemed to be sweating, even in the middle of winter, probably his weight, Dougie had surmised. Dougie had a suspicion of fat people... usually... but the regular driver had always been civil enough, and Dougie was always willing to give a man the benefit of the doubt, even if they were morbidly obese. This new driver was normal-sized, not fat at all, and he wore a thin moustache, looked a bit like a third lip above the other two;

Dougie wondering which pair of lips would do the talking and smiling at his own thought. Driver's hair was brown, with a centre-parting, face was also a bit on the thin side, not especially healthy-looking. The new boarder decided to offer a friendly greeting.

'Mornin.'

The new driver looked at him, or maybe through him... the eyes were a bit odd, didn't seem to focus too well, not a great quality for a bus driver, Dougie thought.

'Haven't seen you before... has the regular driver left?'

Wasn't too chatty this new driver, just kept staring. Maybe he was nervous, maybe this was his first shift on his own... presumably he would have previously driven the route with an experienced hand... if he truly was a new driver. Dougie became aware that he was still waving his "Ridercard", flapping away as if he were trying to scare off a wasp, 'Everything OK?'

The new driver turned his face away to face the road ahead, and then turned back and smiled at Dougie... ah, thought Dougie, progress. Then the smile got a bit too intense, and he wished that the boy would look back at the road again. Happily, this hope was quickly granted. Not a talkative sort, this new driver. Dougie pondered the option of pursuing the fate of the regular driver with the new driver before rapidly deciding not to.

The bus was fairly quiet, nothing unusual there, often quiet this time of the morning. He was heading away from town to his work... everyone else was going in the opposite direction... that suited Dougie... being not great with crowds, he much preferred his own company, and Laura's, of course. On this journey he would happily sit and watch the world go by unless someone else got on and tried to talk to him... hopefully, that would not be the case.

An old fellow with a stick usually boarded at the stop on

Simpson Street, Dougie believed that this fellow was half-mad, always had an "intensity" about him, eyes were a bit bright, luminously blue, and deeply troubled. The two travellers often exchanged hand-waves, but that was definitely the end of it, Dougie being un-keen on developing a friendship, and certainly not with someone whom he believed to be half-mad. Said old gent always disembarked on Welford Road, only three stops further. If it had been him, Dougie would have walked the short distance, but the old fellow was a bit dodgy on his pins, so fair enough, he wouldn't hold that against him. The bus pulled away from the stop as Dougie occupied his regular seat. The guilt of sitting where "you should give up this seat if a disabled person needs it" never went away, but that action had never been required. If it ever did, then sure, Dougie would give up the seat... sitting in the front of the bus just seemed the right place to sit for Dougie. The old fellow who joined at Simpson Street always sat on the other side of the gangway, again where "you should give up this seat if a disabled person needs it". He wasn't disabled, at least not physically, but he was old, so that was pretty much the same thing.

The bus now turned right into Simpson Street. Dougie peered out of the window, you could just about identify what was out of the window, though it could do with a clean, thought Dougie. The stop hove into view, looking slightly fuzzy through the dirt on the outside of the glass. Next to the stop were two ill-defined figures; one was holding a long thin object... that would be the old fellow... the figure, not the long thin object, though the old fellow was also a long thin object. Of the other person, Dougie could not draw any conclusions at this stage, though it did present an outstretched arm for the purpose of hailing the bus, clearly an experienced passenger.

The vehicle slowed and veered in toward the kerb. The doors swung open, and the old fellow clambered up. Process was made easier by the front of the bus sinking, earthbound (driver must have pressed some button)...as new buses do...so the old fellow didn't have a cliff to climb to get on board. Old fellow had an old fellow's pass, of course, and waved it in the vague direction of the driver, who turned toward the new arrival and smiled that "Shining" smile. Old fellow waved his usual wave at Dougie and occupied his regular seat. Dougie waved back. The other customer boarded, a young woman, short, low centre of gravity, brown curly hair. These sorts always seemed to be in a hurry... at least this one was not feeding her ear to a mobile phone. Women like her always seemed even more obsessed with their phones than most. She rushed to the back of the bus and sat down.

Off trundled the bus again, not long to go now. Dougie counted the stops, but he didn't need to; he knew the route by heart, he had the knowledge. Just before the third stop on, the old fellow pressed the bell button and struggled to his feet. Why do these infirms always try and get up way before their stops? Dougie had seen it all before. They struggle to their feet and meander toward the front of the bus, then get thrown about as their stop approaches... just like being on a ship in a storm-tossed sea. Old fellow said something under his breath that might have begun with an "f". For a second, Dougie believed that he heard the driver say something like 'sorry mate,' but quickly realised that he must have been mistaken. Following their earlier encounter, Dougie reasoned it highly unlikely that this driver would converse with a passenger using actual words.

Old fellow disembarked, continuing to mutter something and not waving to Dougie, bus continuing on its way. Young woman with the low centre of gravity took a phone call... ah, Dougie nodded to himself. He had predicted that it would only be a matter of time.

'Yes, yes, I know, I'm not sure what happened, but he was

in a terrible state... couldn't get a word out of him... mind he'd had a lot to drink, yes, yes.'

Then silence, but not quite, the tinny squeak of the other-end caller filling the bus, sounding like radio interference and similarly annoying. Dougie couldn't quite make out what was being said and felt guilt at his own interest, but still strained to listen.

'I think they must have had a row, yes, yes.'

Tinny squeak.

'That's what I thought.'

Tinny squeak.

'I think they made up, hope so anyway.'

Dougie was so concerned about whether they had made up, that he very nearly missed his stop. Fortunately, he happened to look out of the filthy window just as the vaguely familiar shape of the "Old Bell Inn" slid into view. Oops, his stop was coming up, time to press the bell-button.

'I think they'll be OK, seen it all before, yes, yes, that's what Jackie said.'

So, as the final tinny squeak faded away, Dougie dashed off the bus a little more hastily than he would normally have done so.

"DIGITAL SOLUTIONS – YOUR SOFTWARE PARTNER".

This was what the sign said above the entrance to his place of work. "Digital Solutions" lived in a low-rise, not very towering tower block on Gethsemane Street on the very edge of town. This road sat on the outer boundary of the town of Milton, Dougie's hometown... apart from a few very detached houses, there was no further civilisation until you got to Edenston, ten miles down the road.

Inside the building was a foyer of sorts, "DIGITAL SOLU-TIONS – YOUR SOFTWARE PARTNER" was not big enough not to share the building, and so there was a reception that acted for all the occupying businesses, staffed by an operative sat behind a cheap-looking desk. Dougie thought this to be a colossal waste of money as there were rarely any visitors, and those that did appear would be fully aware of where they needed to go, all that was required was decent signage, and the services of the receptionists could be dispensed with. However, he accepted that this would lead to the current team losing their jobs, a situation that made him uncomfortable... and Dougie knew all three of the reception operatives. He was therefore, conflicted. On peering through the stygian gloom of the foyer (two of the lights were out), he noted that Jock was currently on duty. Jock should have been born in Scotland, but this was not the case... in reality, he was a Devonian, Dougie suspecting that some Caledonian blood flowed through the veins of Jock, inherited from way back when. Stout fellow was Jock, steel grey hair, always well turned out, corporate uniform, white shirt and black tie, smart blazer, he was probably ex-military, these chaps always are, not much else to do after you get demobbed.

'Morning, Jock!'

'Hello, Mr Wipton.' Jock considered Dougie to be nice but odd, which was a very accurate assessment.

'Anything exciting happening?'

'Nope.'

Dougie often made pointless *bon-mots* of this sort. Jock was used to them.

'See you later.'

'Aye.'

Dougie made for the lift. "DIGITAL SOLUTIONS" were based on the top floor, floor five. On entering, the lift helpfully informed him that the doors were closing and then, ten seconds later, that they were opening. Out of the lift, down the corridor, sharp left at the end, and there it was in all its glory. "DIGITAL SOLUTIONS," occupying three small offices, each office occupied by one, two or three employees. The three rooms opened off a central hub containing two cosy armchairs and a fish tank. Visitors could sit in the armchairs and look at the fish and would feel calmed as a result. In contrast, Dougie looked at the fish and worried about who was currently feeding them, the "DIGITAL SOLUTIONS TEAM" had committed to sharing the load among themselves, but this plan had probably been decided in a drunken haze at some works' night out. That was why Dougie was worried about the fish.

He walked into his office, the room he shared with Archie (someone else who should have been born in Scotland, in this case, happily, he was). Sharing with only one other person was a consequence of Dougie's seniority in "DIGITAL SOLUTIONS." The next step up was to share an office with a coathanger... like the Boss, Simon Parsons. Archie was away at the moment, off with the missus on a holiday in Tunisia, so, in effect, at this time, Dougie wasn't sharing an office at all. He took advantage of the situation, jacket thrown scandalously across Archie's chair, bag placed provocatively close to Archie's desk. Dougie held nothing back in occupying Archie's personal space while he wasn't there. Office was fine for two, and therefore extremely spacious for one. There would be even more room were it not for the presence of Archie's desk and chair, not to say that Dougie was intending shipping his colleague's stuff out, but the point was worth noting. His own kit was located against the back wall, with a window to the right as he sat down and a shared filing cabinet to the left, largely unused... this was a software development outfit so there wasn't much paper around.

Dougie sat down at his desk and fired up the hardware; he was currently working on a website design for a local school, something a little different from the usual corporate drudgery. He looked at his watch, it was nine-thirty. After working away for a couple of hours, he broke off, as was traditional, at eleven-thirty for a coffee break. "DIGITAL SOLUTIONS" were not big enough to operate a coffee shop, but disaster had been averted in the shape of "ANDERSON ELECTRICS – TRUST THE EXPERTS." This company occupied the first and second floors of the building... and was big enough to run a small catering outlet. "ANDERSON ELECTRICS" were happy for "DIGITAL SOLUTIONS" employees to make use of their facility, yet another example of great British co-operation.

Dougie headed for the stairs, content to descend manually. He had made a conscious decision some time back to only take the lift when ascending. The coffee place was basically a serving hatch in the second-floor lobby. Although "ANDERSON ELECTRICS" was larger than "DIGITAL SOLUTIONS," they were not exactly FTSE fodder, and so the existence of catering, modest as it was, was unusual. Dougie recalled that the "ANDERSON ELECTRICS" Chairman had bought into some crazy "Worker Contentment" cult, placing the well-being of hard-working employees at the very core of the company, probably an American idea, Dougie had assumed, but Alleluia for that. If the largess of a stateside business guru ensured the availability of morning coffee for himself, he was truly grateful.

The serving lady, Helen, had become almost a friend to Dougie, having worked behind the hatch for ages, and since she was rarely overrun with customers, she and Dougie had indulged in many a blether down the years. Dougie wasn't one for opening up to folk, but he had, on occasion, spilt some pretty personal beans to Helen and her to him. A year back, she had encountered stormy domestic waters, had almost split with Jerry (her husband), and all of it had come out to Dougie. He had been quite proud that she had confided in him and had tried to say all the right things. Maybe it had worked because the storm did pass, and they were still together... possibly he, Dougie, had helped to save a marriage. This very thought had grown him by an inch.

Dougie sauntered toward the serving hatch, checking that he had change. Helen never had enough change, and so, although the price of his coffee was one pound and the easy option would be for him to hand over a one-pound coin, he would always try to pay in smaller change... to help her out. Having convinced himself that he was sufficiently equipped, he raised his head and rapidly ascertained that the frame of the hatch was empty. It was clearly open for business, the light was on, and Ken Bruce was crooning out of the radio (though only quietly so as not to disturb the hard workers of "ANDERSON ELECTRICS" in the nearby offices). Suddenly a figure popped up, obviously Helen had been carrying out some task, out-of-sight beneath the counter.

'Morning Hel... oh!'

Not Helen.

Dougie's mind shook a little at this. It had always been Helen. This non-Helen situation was most unwelcome.

'Sorry, I thought you were Helen.'

Stupid thing to say.

Then Dougie had another brain-shake moment.

This woman was the low centre of gravity woman, the woman on the bus, the 'yes-yes' woman, short, curly brown hair, the lot.

The woman smiled. She wore the uniform of Helen, a kind of blue overall, but she wasn't Helen. Different clothes from when Dougie had seen her on the bus, she must have changed. Couldn't remember what she had been wearing on the bus, but it wasn't the blue overall unless it was under a coat; he simply couldn't remember.

'Hello.' He repeated.

Hard to know how to act in the face of persistent smiling, Dougie decided to smile back.

Eventually, the low centre of gravity woman stopped smiling and used her mouth to speak actual words.

'What can I get you?'

'Coffee, please.'

'Certainly.'

Dougie wondered whether he should raise the issue of their shared bus journey.

'Were you on the forty-five bus this morning?'

'No.'

'It's just that....'

'Anything else?'

'No thanks, still one pound?'

'Yes.'

Dougie handed over a handful of coins, all carefully counted out in advance, to the sum of one pound.

'Thanks, help yourself to milk and sugar.'

No recognition that he was paying in small change as a favour. The mug (yes, a mug, no disposable cups here) full of the steaming life-giver was placed on the counter.

Dougie took the mug, 'OK if I bring the mug back after I'm done?' He almost added... 'Helen had always been fine with that', but didn't, instead asking, 'By the way, where is Helen today, day off?' This was clearly nonsense. Helen had never had a day off, or more accurately a morning off, the counter closing at thirteen-hundred.

The yes-yes woman confined herself to the first question, 'We close at one, the mug has to be back by then, or it won't get washed up.'

'I know.'

Dougie waited for a response to his second question... response came there none, and so he tried again, from a slightly different direction.

'I can't remember Helen ever having time off.'

'Really?'

'No.'

Dougie, never the most patient individual, was finding this

exchange increasingly trying, 'I mean, is she OK? She's not ill, is she?'

'I've no idea. I don't know her.'

'But... but you must, surely... don't you work for the same people.'

'Don't know what you mean... now, I must get on.'

The woman withdrew through a door behind the counter, leaving a frustrated but coffee-equipped customer denied a further enquiry. Dougie went back to his desk, shaking his head for most of the short journey... so distracted was he that he used the stairs and not the lift. He had no intention of returning the empty mug on this occasion. A further encounter with the new server was not required. No... he would wait until Helen came back.

As a rule, Dougie would work through from coffee until thirteen-hundred (delivering his empty mug back to the hatch at about twelve-fifteen, though not this time, of course, not wishing to interact with the Helen-replacement). Generally, for lunch, he would head out of the building to a sandwich shop just round the corner... no reason for today to be any different in that regard, despite his bad experience at the coffee hatch. At some point in the recent past, he had contemplated asking the "ANDERSON ELECTRICS" people whether they had ever considered extending the opening hours of their catering operation to encompass lunch (his lunch that is, beginning thirteen-hundred). This would, of course, entail offering food... sandwiches, rolls, etc., which they currently did not. This thought had come to nought, and so he had remained a customer of "SANDWICH CITY."

As he had correctly predicted earlier that morning, the rain had come, not too hard at present, merely a soft drizzle, but the sky was full of more. Dougie, having reached the foyer, peered outside and instantly retreated to his office; there was his emergency umbrella. Dougie kept an umbrella in the house (several in fact, but two of them belonged to Laura), also one at his work... you can never be over-prepared when it comes to the English weather. All he had to do was to remember to return each umbrella to its correct station after use, which he always did.

'Bit damp outside, Mr Wipton,' said Jock, almost at the end of his shift.

'I've come well-armed!'

Suitably equipped, Dougie polished off the journey to "SANDWICH CITY" in no time at all. Upon opening the door to the small shop, he looked across at the counter, expecting to see the usual face, or at least one of the usual faces, ready and willing to serve. The business was owned and run by a husband-and-wife team, Gary and Margaret, middle-aged, hard-working, friendly sorts. Normally only one of them would be on duty at any given time, rotating in a predictable way, Margaret... Gary... Margaret... Gary, etc., etc. Dougie recalled that, on the previous day, Gary had served him a tuna-mayo baguette, so today he was fully expecting Margaret (never Maggie) to be in place.

Dougie didn't know too much about driving buses, but he naively imagined that your typical bus driver would be a bus driver and nothing else, no other employment required or permitted. Surely there would be a full roster of shifts to occupy your typical bus driver; that was what Dougie thought. This misconception made it all the more surprising for Dougie as he stared at the new-driver, first encountered on his journey to work that very morning. Dougie tried not to stare as a rule, but in this case, it was probably justified.

'Er...'

'Sorry.'

'Oh!'

'Can I get you something?' The new-driver come sand-wich-salesman smiled... with that familiar new-driver smile in the familiar thin face. He wasn't wearing the bus-driver uniform now, of course, merely a standard white shirt, must have changed clothes.

'Sorry. Haven't I seen you somewhere before?'

'It's a small world, so quite possibly.'

'Sorry, it's just that... well, I'm so used to seeing Margaret or Gary in here...'

That smile again, Dougie had hope that his mention of the owners would prompt some sort of reaction/confession but no luck there.

'Can I get you something?' New-driver came again. 'I can do you a nice tuna-mayo baguette?' Dougie wasn't too focussed on baguettes. Strange ideas were beginning to crystallise in his mind... or maybe fears... he remembered his dad recounting stories of the "odd behaviour", of *his* father, Dougie's grandad, whom he had never met. Apparently, this relative had suffered from some psychotic condition that had required detention in secure accommodation at one point. Dougie had always believed that this sort of thing could be genetic, and therefore could be passed down through the generations... as it were.

'Well... can I get you something... anything?' New-driver was sounding desperate, desperate to sell a tuna-mayo ba-guette, or any baguette.

'Yes, I'll have one of those.'

Dougie wouldn't normally have the same baguette filling on successive days, but the unexpected appearance of new-driver was affecting his judgement.

'Ah... good choice... do you want butter... or spread?'

'No, no thanks.'

'I almost forgot to ask, white or brown?'

After what had happened that morning, with new-driver,

and the yes-yes woman, maybe he was in the middle of some mental short-circuit. He didn't feel mad, but then... what does being mad actually feel like? What specific variety of madness led to you seeing the same people over and over again?

'I said, brown or white?'

'Brown.'

Maybe it was just some sort of weird whatever... some people do look like some other people. He himself probably looked a bit like someone else. New-driver hummed as he made up the roll, happy to be busy.

'Anything else?'

'A can of "Sprite" please.'

'Certainly, that will be, let's see now, that will be... baguette is two-pound fifty and the can is a pound, so that'll be...'

Dougie was already handing him the money, didn't bother with the correct amount on this occasion as "SANDWICH CITY" rarely experienced issues with change, so a five pound note was tendered,

'Thanks.'

'Thank you. I'll just get the drink for you... I suspect you would prefer a cold one?'

Dougie didn't much care but off the fellow went to look in the fridge, only to return empty-handed, 'Really sorry, but we don't seem to have any cold "Sprites", looks like the fridge hasn't been stocked up, just can't get the staff you know.'

'Who would normally stock the fridge?'

'I can let you have one that's been on the shelf?'

Dougie accepted this proposition, neglecting to pursue his question.

'Thanks.'

'Will there be anything else?' The query remained unanswered as Dougie had already turned to leave, words left hanging in the foody-smelling air of the shop.

He was feeling a little light-headed now, almost like a caffeine rush. Maybe yes-yes woman had made a stronger than expected brew earlier. Exiting "SANDWICH CITY" in a bit of a daze, he was too distracted to notice the rain, the umbrella remaining furled. He did manage to note, however, that Jock had stood down by the time he got back, John One now being on duty. The identifier was necessary as there were two Johns, with this John the more human of the two, John Two was in a state of permanent misery and made sure that the whole world knew it, he was the older of the two Johns, but that was no excuse in Dougie's eyes. John One was in his forties, dark-haired and respectably bespectacled, slightly less smart than Jock. Instead of a tie, he sported an open-necked shirt, standards not quite those of Jock's, maybe not an ex-soldier.

'Afternoon Mr Wipton.'

'Hello, John.'

Dougie meandered past the desk, 'Everything OK, Mr Wipton?'

'Er fine, just fine.'

'It's just that you look a little distracted. Everything OK?'

'I said everything is just fine.'

'Sorry, it's just that you look a little distracted.'

Dougie began to question his view of the merits of the two Johns... and then realised the error of his ways, 'Sorry John, don't mean to appear snippy, been a... strange morning.'

Dougie had only been back in "his" office for half an hour, having consumed the baguette and drunk the drink, when the phone rang.

'Douglas Wipton.' Sounded better than Dougie.

'Ah Dougie, Simon, I need to come and speak to you about... something, have you got a mo'?' Simon didn't sound too much like Simon, but this passed Dougie by... still trying to get his head round all the coincidences.

'Of course, Simon, no problem, are you coming over now?'

'I'll be there in five minutes.'

Dougie sank back into his chair, slowly, a smile growing into his face. The mind behind had accepted it all, accepted that a couple of people that he had met looked uncommonly like a couple of other people, or maybe, just maybe, they *were* the other people, big deal. The alternative explanation was that he, Dougie, was a bit mad, and he didn't believe that this was the case. Footsteps evolved, growing closer, there was a knock on the door.

'Come in!'

The office door opened, and new-driver entered, smiling. Simon Parsons, his boss, or "line-manager" as he was more correctly branded, had been replaced by the personage of the bus driver/sandwich seller, again in different garb. In the guise of bus driver, he had worn the company uniform, as a sandwich seller he had worn the company uniform, but now, as Dougie's boss, he was... wearing the company uniform... but this time it was collar and tie, not a "MILTONBUS" label in sight.

'Hi Dougie, thanks for making time. I need to speak to you about the Price contract; we are getting some pressure to complete ahead of schedule... how close are you to completion?'

Bizarrely Dougie continued to operate normally, maybe his senses had been so pummelled that they had gone into undead mode. His mind turned forensically to the Price contract... truth was, he had put it to one side so that he could get the school job done.

'Er, well, the thing is Simon...' Hell, this man was not Simon Parsons. Why was he calling him Simon? 'Thing is...'

Behind the rational exchange, justifications and excuses

drifted away as sick reality sank over Dougie's world, the coincidence theory was out of the window, and so what did that leave?

'What are you trying to say, Dougie?'

'Everything is fine... I'll have the Price work done by the end of the week.'

New-driver smiled again, 'That's good news, but...,' and at this, the thing that had replaced Simon Parsons placed his face firmly at the centre of Dougie's field of vision, 'It has to happen, Dougie... you mustn't let me down.'

The breath of new-driver wafted unwelcomingly across Dougie's face, 'No, no, it will be done,' he replied, beginning to perspire very slightly.

'Good, good, well done!' Simon new-driver gave him a comradely slap across the shoulder, 'We'll speak tomorrow... see how you're getting on.'

Dougie was alone again. Suddenly he wished, he very much wished, that Archie was not away in Tunisia but instead was here, in the office. Then again, what if Archie was here and looked like new-driver? That would be awful, so maybe it was for the best that he wasn't here. Dougie nodded out loud.

He usually broke off at fifteen-hundred and went outside for a wander, just for ten minutes or so, just to break the routine. Today he didn't feel much like it... wasn't in the mood, carried on working until seventeen-hundred.

On one previous occasion, Dougie had gone to the pub on his way home from work, that had been about two years ago, and had been celebratory. "DIGITAL SOLUTIONS" had won an award for its "Contribution to Community", some work that largely, he, Dougie, had carried out for a local sports club... done it mostly off his own back and in his own time.

To mark the occasion, he had tried to drum up a crowd to

visit the local for a knees-up. Everyone had thought it a great plan, and nobody went... nobody except Dougie, he had decided to damn them all and go anyway, by himself, and he did. After consuming a couple of beers very quickly, he had gone home, a little late and slightly inebriated... Laura had been most forgiving if memory served him correctly. On this occasion, Dougie thought a pint might help him understand what had been going on... a primitive male reaction, utterly nonsensical but also eminently justifiable... given the circumstances. He put on his jacket and turned out the light, the umbrella was not needed as it had stopped raining. Looking round the office just prior to departure, he wondered what tomorrow would bring.

The pub in question was a short walk away from the workplace, maybe fifteen minutes for a rapid mover such as Dougie. He considered phoning Laura... to tell her that he would be late, but then thought better of it... he would just think up some excuse, make it sound like an emergency, some crisis at work, 'unavoidably detained', that sort of thing. During the short trek to the "Gardener's Arms", he passed one new-driver and one yes-yes woman. The first was clearly a decorator of some sort, dressed in overalls liberally treated with varieties of paint. The second, the woman, was in casuals. Dougie couldn't guess what she did for a living; maybe she was a mother and a wife, maybe she had a family somewhere, just like the yes-yes woman that ran the "ANDERSON ELECTRICS" coffee bar might have had... or the yes-yes woman on the bus, long ago, that morning.

Dougie knew exactly what was coming next, as he swung open the door to the "Gardener's" and stepped inside, into the dark. This was a "traditional" boozer with a public bar (snug), to the left and a lounge (best room), to the right. Dougie turned to the left. The bar counter itself shone like a lighthouse in the gloom of the room... as a ship in peril, he navigated through treacherous tables to reach the safety of the light.

A bar-tender appeared. Dougie jumped back a step, startled, the reason being he had never seen this man before. No new-driver here.

'What can I get you mate?'

'Pedigree.'

'Pint or half?'

Daft question, thought Dougie, 'Pint... please.'

'Anything else?'

'Not right now.'

'Three-fifty, please.'

Dougie scrabbled round in his pockets and dug out the requisite change, happened to have the correct amount.

'Thanks.'

On turning round, he noticed two new-drivers and a yes-yes woman, all sitting separately at various sites around the small bar. Dougie positioned himself out of harm's way in a corner.

Dougie was no authority on mental illness. However, he was minded, once again, to consider whether he might be going out of his mind in some fashion. He had earlier dismissed this hypothesis but surely there could only be so many coincidences and so, being a curious sort, began to muse on what his illness might be called.

'Ow's it goin'?'

Shit... one of the new-drivers wanted to be friends.

'As I aways says... as I aways says, if a man is on 'is own in a pub... then 'e must be lookin' for compny.'

The new-driver in question had risen from his seat at the next table... and wandered across, eventually, in so doing, describing a sort of Brownian motion, 'Ow's it going?'

'Not bad, long day at work, you know the sort of thing.'

'Nah, not really... 'aven't worked for ten year, back's gone, y'see, been on the sick for ten year.'

'Sorry to hear it.'

'Does 'ave its compensations, don' 'ave to work, that's one of 'em.'

'I see.'

Dougie tried to study this unwanted visitor. Did he really look like the others, really?

Yes was the answer, different clothes (shabby), different person... but the same body, and the same 'third-lip' moustache.

New-driver sat down, or more accurately, collapsed down, onto a seat at Dougie's table.

'Can I get you another one, ga'an, 'ave another one?'

'No thanks... I should go home... wife waiting, rolling pin, you know the sort of thing...'

'Nah... divorced... couldn't put up with the wife's drinkin'.' This king of comedy then roared with inebriation.

At that very moment, inside of Dougie's head, a tiny pixie changed something, not very much, but enough, he stared at this man, this intrusive bastard, 'You see him, him over there...?'

He pointed at the other new-driver, sitting alone at a table in the centre of the room. This sudden request led to some eye-widening on the part of his unwelcome companion, 'Eh?'

'Him, over there, he looks exactly like you, look at him... look?' Voice volume increasing by just enough to notice, Dougie pointed in a jabby sort of way, accusatory.

'Nah, nothing like me.'

Dougie suddenly stood up, he was about to cause a scene, first time for everything, he, Dougie, causing a scene in a pub, what would Laura say? He grabbed this new-driver by the upper arm and pulled him to his feet. This was a risk, of course, and this initiative might conceivably have led to a fight, an event that Dougie was singularly ill-prepared to handle, but these were strange times. Happily, the potential punch did not materialise, neither did any serious resistance.

'I'm Dougie. What's your name?' Dougie enquired as he gently dragged the forlorn and totally innocent regular new-driver across the room.

'Joe.'

'Pleased to meet you, Joe.'

His actions had already begun to attract attention. Dougie felt the eyes of the barman upon him... he would need to be quick. Presently he and his companion arrived at the table of the second new-driver, who was still staring at the space just in front of his face.

'Joe, I'd like to introduce you to... I'm sorry, sir, I don't know your name?'

Second new-driver raised his head and looked blankly at his inquisitor. There didn't appear to be any significant signs of very much there in terms of a response or recognition.

'Sorry?'

Dougie was enjoying himself, but he was pretty much off his head by now, though he'd had hardly had a sip, it was all adrenaline, and it couldn't last. Dougie was about to fight the law, and the law was about to win. The bar-tender drifted into the edge of his field of vision, then moved remorselessly inwards until finally, he could not be ignored.

'Sorry, sir, I think you've probably had enough, time to go home.'

Barman was secretly cursing himself for serving this guy... yet he had seemed sober enough when he first came in.

Dougie Wipton was in the process of being ejected from a public house. Stop the presses.

'Do you see these two men here?' Dougie ranted, sounding very much like a man who had had too much, 'Do you not think that they look exactly the same?'

'Of course they do, sir... now, if you wouldn't mind stepping this way.'

Dougie was assisted to the nearest exit by means of a firm grip on his lower left arm.

'This is ridiculous...'

'Good night, sir.'

And so it was that Dougie found himself outside the "Gardener's Arms", wondering when the next bus was due. He looked at his watch. It was eighteen hundred, not too late, guilty-child syndrome.

There was a stop a few minutes walk away. The forty-five wasn't an option, but Dougie fancied that the thirty-four passed by these parts... it would mean a short walk at the other end, but he needed to get home. A yes-yes woman walked by as he headed for the stop, but he barely noticed. As he glanced at the houses to his right, a new-driver stared out of a window at him as he passed. A young child, presumably the son of new-driver, appeared alongside as Dougie slipped out of vision. At the bus stop, Dougie peered at the timetable, the print size was impossibly small, but after much squinting, Dougie discovered that a thirty-four was due in the next fifteen minutes.

Following a short wait, sure, enough, here was the blue and white beast, Dougie had always thought the local bus livery quite attractive, but this consideration wasn't at the forefront of his mind at this time. Sticking out an arm did the job, the ship coming ashore, then he was on-board and away. The driver was a stranger, much to Dougie's surprise, but there were multiple yes-yes women and new-drivers scattered around in the lower saloon.

Dougie's rage had passed. He was never one for rage. A mood of acceptance had moved in to replace it, and beyond that, a sense of understanding, some wonderful realisation slowly germinating in some place within his mind, that he had not previously accessed. All seemed to be associated with memories of the dream from the previous night, which were gradually squeezing themselves in. Dougie opened the door to these thoughts.

'Come right in'.

'Well, you're heading in the right direction. Sure enough you are.'

'Dougie was on the road to the world of the utter calm, the land of what will be, will be, the island of destiny unchallengeable... carried by the number thirty-four.

He was soon off the bus at Luke Street, two streets and several new-drivers/yes-yes women from the house... Dougie didn't care. Dougie was very close to understanding.

He almost ran home, not quite, and he was smiling by the time he got there.

'Hi, sorry I'm late.'

Laura was in the hall, 'Dougie, it's quarter-to seven.'

'I know.'

She gave him a hug, 'Everything OK? I was worried. You should have phoned.'

'I know, sorry.'

'You know that I worry when you're late, you're hardly ever late.'

'Sorry.'

'Have you had anything to eat?'

'Not really.'

'It's quite late. I had my dinner ages ago.'

Thanks very much, thought Dougie. 'I bet you're hungry again, aren't you?'

Laura's gaze was neutral. More information required.

'I fancy some fish and chips. Could you manage some fish and chips?'

'I wouldn't mind a small portion of chips.' She replied, face full of questions.

'I'll go and get some, won't be long.'

'Why are you so late, Dougie?'

'Just had some stuff to finish off at work, won't be long.'
Dougie was off again, off to the local chippy only ten minutes'
walk away.

Did he really understand? Did he... Dougie Wipton, know
what the hell was going on? This was a question that he
addressed as he headed chippy-wards. The streets were fairly
quiet this time of night, but he did pass a couple of yes-yes
women and at least one new-driver. The world was strangely
bright, oddly light... more so than was proper at this time of
year, it was still summertime, just, but by this stage he would
have expected the first signs of dusk to be apparent. Dougie
peered at the sun away to the West. It was high in the sky, far
too high for August, at this time of the evening, thought
Dougie. It was probably where it should be at about three
o'clock, thought Dougie, all very rationally.

In ten minutes, he found himself at the "JOLLY FRIAR."
Inside there was a short queue, mostly men (new-drivers), but
there was one woman, not a yes-yes woman, a real bonafide,
normal woman. Dougie smiled at her, and she smiled back.
Was she even aware of the situation?

'Hello, I hope you don't mind me asking but don't you
think it's strange that everyone else in the queue looks the
same?'

Normal woman looked a little uncomfortable, 'Can't say
I've noticed.'

Dougie felt like suggesting that maybe she should take a
look but instead fell silent as he waited for his turn to be
served. The man behind the counter was a thin-lipped new-
driver, dressed in white overalls, looking the part of a chippy-
maestro, 'What can I get you?'

'Fish and chips, and a portion of chips, please.' Said
Dougie.

'Salt and vinegar?'

'Yes, please.'

Off he went, humming away, but before he was out of earshot, Dougie asked him a question.

'Excuse me, don't you think it strange that all the men in the queue look like you.'

'Lucky people.'

Two greasy paper parcels were placed on the hot, glass counter. Dougie picked them up, chip-oil already leaking, made him wish that he'd brought a bag with him.

'Excuse me, do you have a plastic bag?'

'Fraid not.'

Never mind, thought Dougie, only ten minutes' walk to home. As he walked up the street, he noted that it was still high daytime... at half-past seven. The sun didn't appear to have moved at all since late afternoon, stuck in the sky, at about forty-five degrees or thereabouts. Dougie smiled.

'Might meet some other folk on the way. My advice to you is to be polite and wish them well.'

'Dougie, Dougie!'

Laura was waiting outside the house on the main road as Dougie sauntered towards her, clutching chips in bags.

'What's up?'

'Look!' An arm lanced out and pointed skywards, 'Look... the sun, it's still where it was hours ago, what's going on!?'

'Why don't we put "The BBC News Channel" on? We can watch it while we eat our chips.'

Dougie knew exactly what would be on the "News Channel", well, actually he didn't... but he did know exactly what would not be on it. Laura fired up the remote as they lay back in their respective chairs. She stared as the screen came to life.

'... And Jamie is obviously a very happy cat. Just look at him smiling.'

It was a programme about cats.

Dougie tucked into his fish and chips, smiling inwardly, 'The end of time doesn't seem especially newsworthy.'

'What?'

'I said... the end of time...'

'I heard you.' Laura's voice was just a little strangled.

'If the sun stops moving, then that is the end of time.'

Laura didn't say anything, and so Dougie just carried on talking.

'Your chips are getting cold.' He said.

Laura still wasn't saying anything... or eating the chips.

After a minute or two, she rose, placed the bag of remaining chips on a side table, and departed the lounge.

Dougie gave her a few minutes, gave him time to finish his food, then went a-hunting... she was in the garden, the plot bathed in golden light from a young sun, so full of energy and with so much to give.

He stood very close to her so that he could wrap an arm round her shoulder.

'Sorry about that.'

'Sorry about what?'

Dougie wasn't clear what he was sorry about and so simply smiled... and then looked at his shoes.

'You know, don't you?'

'Sorry?'

'You know what's happening, I know you, Dougie Wipton, when you know a secret, you always come over all sarcastic and smug.'

Dougie looked at the sky, 'Maybe.'

'So, what's going on?'

'You won't believe me.'

'Ach!'

'Let's go back inside. I'm getting overheated out here.'

Once inside, Dougie told his wife what he thought was

happening; it didn't take long. She listened. By the time he had finished talking, it was past nine o'clock.

They returned to the garden, Dougie had dug out his sunglasses. The sun burned with its new life, filling the entire sky with yellow flame. A blackbird sang to the world from a nearby chestnut tree.

'Beautiful, isn't it?'

Laura simply stood and tried to understand.

'We should go to bed.'

'But it's still...'

'Light? We can't wait for it to get dark, Laura. We need to be sharp for tomorrow.'

It seemed odd going to bed in the middle of the day. The bedroom was equipped with heavy-duty curtains, but the power of the solar light was still all around as they turned in. Laura could not sleep, the glow filtering through the curtains filling her closed eyes as the clock-hours ticked by, ten, eleven, twelve. Still it was light.

Dougie slept the sleep of one who thought he knew.

He awoke alone. Laura was already up and about... jumping out of bed, he pulled the curtains aside. There was the garden, under the same sun, in the same place. Dougie stretched his arms to the heavens.

Laura came into the bedroom.

'Morning!'

'I didn't sleep a wink.'

'I know.'

They had breakfast, Dougie munched away on his "Shredded Wheat", good to have his cereal back. Laura picked at a round of toast.

'You should eat something.'

'Not hungry.'

'You should still eat something.'

Laura smiled weakly.

Dougie washed the breakfast things, whistling away.

'Are you going to work?'

'No, what's the point?'

Laura screwed up her face, 'But you can't just... not go to work.'

'Just watch me. We'll go for a walk instead.'

Dougie and Laura went for a walk, locking the door as they left the house, pointlessly, thought Dougie.

They wandered down Adam Park Road. It was nine-thirty.

There was no life on Adam Park Road. Cars were parked in driveways, the carriageway empty of all traffic, even buses. Dougie glanced at the houses as they passed, some lights were on in the rooms within, but there were no people, no people.

The "SPAR" shop round the corner on Adam Place was always open, even on Christmas Day! But not on this day. The shop was dark and closed.

'There's no-one, nobody anywhere.' Laura murmured.

'That's right.'

They walked on... no-one waited at the bus stop, the tiny "community library" on Blake Street was closed.

But the sun still beamed down, and it was still hot.

'Shall we go home?'

'Yes.'

And so they walked back home, just the two of them, the only two left.

Back into the house.

'I think we should go into the garden.'

'Yes.'

They went through into the garden. It was so beautiful, so perfect, so... new.

Dougie looked at the apple tree, full to bursting with ripe-red fruit.

He turned to Laura.

'Now do you understand?'

Laura wasn't sure.

'What are you talking about, Dougie?'

'Fancy one of those apples, but we probably shouldn't... can't make the same mistake again.'

By this point, Laura was lost... lost in the lunacy of her husband, yet at the same time overwhelmed by something...

'Ever seen any snakes in the garden, Laura? You know that we have several species in the UK, Smooth, Adder, Grass?'

'We don't have any snakes in our garden, Dougie. What are you talking about?'

'In that case, everything will be just fine. It will be OK this time round, won't make the same mistakes again.'

~ The ~
Devil
in the
Rainbow

It was very cold on that morning.

Very cold on that December morning, standing amid the raw stones of H'ell Tor.

With the sun low in the East, as red as ever it was, and twice as big and out-of-focus behind the curtain of the air, the light was very young on that morning. Light not strong enough to make the stones live, and so they slumbered in the semi-dark as the man stood among them. Dark they may be, yet they were still the friends of the man, the only friends that were left. The only friends left standing, here, high atop the granite mass of Dartmoor with quiet all around, wind still sleeping, night creatures away to roost, day creatures yet to rise. The man, a tall man, a very strong man... a powerful man, square-shouldered man, short hair, fiercely short hair, brown eyes blinking in the almost-light as the sun climbed so very slowly and the shadows of the stones grew closer to their masters.

Dark man, still as the stone, looked back and down at the snow on the ground, a fine layer of snow on the ground, saw what was there and smiled, smiled great regret.

First day of the holidays was as good as it got.

This was it, Monday... not really the first day of the Christmas holiday, that had been Saturday, but Saturday was the weekend and so didn't really count.

So, this was the first day then.

Aiden Sweet opened his eyes, good and proper, thoughts turning to the prospect of getting out of bed... then closing his eyes again because this was the first day of the holiday, and he had been working very hard, and he deserved...

'Aiden, are you intending to get up any time soon?'

Thoughts of laying in, undetected, below the radar, crushed by the call of the wild... Mother.

How to respond?

'In a minute!'

Would she hear? The reply might have been muffled by the duvet... he didn't really care... this was the first day of the holiday, after all. Oh no! That was the sound of her coming up the stairs; maybe she hadn't heard. If she had, then she clearly hadn't been put off. Needed to up the volume.

'I'll be down in a minute!'

Too late, the door was opening. She was coming in.

'Do you know what the time is?'

There she stood, small mousy Mum, Mum with the brown hair, a little like his own, though he didn't have his in the style of a ponytail. Mum with the kindly blue eyes that always seemed to be too large for her face... reminded him of a very friendly yet indefinable cartoon character. Mum, full of energy. Mum against the world and the world better look out because my Mum is coming to get you.

'I said... Do you know what the time is?'

Hard not to feel soothed by the lilting Devonian tones, Mum sounded calm even when she was angry... maybe she was never truly angry... Aiden really thought this to be true.

'Sorry, Mum. I'll get up right now.'

'It's nearly ten o'clock, I could ask if you want any breakfast, but it's nearly lunchtime!'

'Sorry.'

'I don't mind you having a little lie-in in the holidays, but it's ten o'clock... nearly.'

'Sorry.'

'Well... Do you want any breakfast?'

'Er... no, I think I'll wait until lunch.'

'You should eat something... I'll make you some toast... would you like some toast... If I made you some toast, would you eat it?'

How could someone with such a gentle voice convey so much impatience so effectively? That was a gift that only Mums possessed.

'That would be nice.'

'Well, get up and come downstairs...'

And then, as she had turned to leave through the still-open door of the bedroom.

'... I've got something to show you.'

That voice, shorn of the burden of the everyday, now imparted a sense of mystery, and that mystery was picked up by the young Aiden Sweet.

'What?'

'I'll show you when you come downstairs.'

With that, she had gone, leaving the sense of mystery suspended in the air... more than sufficient to raise a sixteen-year-old boy from his holiday bed.

*

Up and out, Aiden exited his small but beloved bedroom, with its wardrobe and desk and its view of the moor from the tiny window, and headed for the bathroom. Time to begin preparations for the day and to be shown something by his mum, something mysterious. Aiden peered at himself in the mirror in the bathroom, as young boys were wont to do, maybe to look and see if anything had changed since the last time.

No, it hadn't.

Still the same short, brown, wispy hair, and the blue eyes, smaller than Mum's, and the elongated face, just like Mum's. Unlike Mum, he was quite tall for his age, don't know where that came from... Dad had been tall, yes, that would be it. It would have come from his Dad, maybe from his Dad's Dad, or his Dad's Mum, or something like that. A tall, slim Aiden Sweet looked back at Aiden Sweet from inside the looking glass as the face was washed and the teeth were cleaned, and then it was time to get dressed for the day, for the first real day of holiday, and to go downstairs, and to be shown something mysterious by his Mum.

Cleaning and dressing all done in the tiny bathroom. Everything was tiny in this house... it was a tiny house. On this floor, the upstairs floor, there was his tiny bedroom and the even tinier bathroom and Mum's room. Mum's room was the biggest upstairs room, but not by much. All the upstairs rooms led to a tiny space at the top of the stairs, and that is where Aiden now stood, at the take-off point for the trip to downstairs. The stairs were steep, and each step was very high, and so great care was required to effect a safe descent. This fact, Aiden knew, but he took no notice of it, didn't need to. He'd made the journey plenty enough times. At the bottom was a kind of hallway. Directly in front of Aiden lay the principal entrance of the house, leading out to the front garden, to the right, the kitchen, door beside a vertiginous grandfather clock that had descended from some distant ancestor, and which continued to sing the chimes of the hour, a voice to be heard all over the house at the appointed times.

Once at ground level, Aiden rapidly determined that Mum was in the kitchen. Aiden could hear the Mum-noise, the sound of cupboards being closed, of things being moved around and put on tables, and then taken off again. The smell of toasting bread percolated through the gaps around the closed door in expectation of his arrival downstairs. The door to the left provided admittance to the "front room" or the lounge, or the sitting room... and the dining room because there was no separate dining room. Downstairs did host another room, the room behind the kitchen, but that room was not "lived-in" as such. It was too small to be of any real use, apart from as a repository for items that no-one really cared anything about.

'Is that you, Aiden?' Mum shouted from the kitchen. 'Your toast is ready... Do you want any marmalade with it?'

'Yes, please,' conversation continuing through the closed kitchen door. The door then opened, and there she was again.

'About time... go onto the front room and I'll bring it in... Do you want some tea?'

'Yes, that would be nice... What was it that you wanted to show me?'

Mum smiled a mysterious smile.

'Wait until you have had your breakfast.'

'Is it a bird?'

Aiden thought that the mysterious thing might be a bird. Both he and Mum were keen bird watchers. They often went out together in the holidays, or at weekends, armed with Mum's posh binoculars, to try and spot something unusual, maybe a bullfinch... they had seen a bullfinch a month or so ago... not while on any kind of grand expedition, merely wandering in the garden... there it was, sitting on a branch in the lilac bush at the edge of the plot, next to the front gate, large as life. Aiden had seen it first, almost close enough to touch, no binoculars necessary. Mum had said 'well done,' and they had tried to take a photo with Mum's posh camera, but the blasted thing had flown away.

Mum did not reply to Aiden's question, instead retreating silently to the kitchen, Aiden reluctantly migrating to the front room to await the toast and marmalade. It seemed to take forever to arrive. Had he any inkling of what the "thing" was that he was to be shown, he might have been able to jump the gun, to discover it for himself, but he didn't, and so he couldn't, and he would just have to wait. Certainly, it was the case that the front room looked as it always had and so whatever it was, wasn't in here.

Front room was a very light room, light and airy, despite being tiny, cream-wallpapered and a kind of grey-that-wasn't really, but that was the closest colour, carpet. There was a dining table of sorts, leastways a table that was used as a dining table, a table with two chairs, two chairs being sufficient for the current population of the house. The front room was also home to a settee (or sofa), two armchairs, an old television, a rather grand cabinet (known as the china cabinet... because it contained china, not because it had come from that country), a chest of drawers, and a birdcage, next to the window that presented garden views. The cage was occupied by a green and yellow budgerigar, name of Bobby, that chirped constantly and regularly sent Mum up the wall.

'I'm going to kill it, if it doesn't shut up, I... I will kill it.'

She hadn't thus far, and so Bobby endured.

There had once been two budgies... Joey had gone AWOL a year ago, executing a daring bid for freedom by flying out through the open window of the front room during an authorised exercise period outside of his cell. Joey had never been seen again. Aiden had been concerned that his (or her, didn't know which) close friend, Bobby, would pine for his/her lost companion, but that situation, happily, had not transpired, Bobby taking it on the chin... or the beak, if you will. Indeed, Bobby now appeared committed to generating enough noise for the two of them. The breakfast guest now took a seat at the table impatiently.

'Here we are,' Mum was back, carrying a tray adorned with toast and tea... once the cargo was safely deposited on the table, Aiden tried again.

'What is it that you want to show me? Can't you tell me?'

Mum smiled again, definitely enjoying this, thought Aiden. Definitely enjoying making me suffer. How bad was that? Your own Mum prepared to inflict such distress on her own son.

How bad was that?

'The quicker you eat your breakfast, the quicker you will know.'

Now she was trying to initiate indigestion as well.

How bad was that?

Mum switched on the radio that lurked on top of the chest of drawers. It was a digital radio that should surely be quite small... this was Aiden's belief... but this digital radio was huge, looked to Aiden bigger than those old-fashioned radios that he had seen in pictures. Music bathed the room as Aiden launched into the toast... Radio Two... middle-of-the-road. That suited Aiden, musical middle-of-the-road was absolutely fine with him. This may well be anomalous for a lad of his age, but too bad. Toast was consumed at express pace, interspersed with gulps of hot tea. Mum looked on with her head on one side, a little like Bobby in the cage, who, unusually, was currently silent.

'You shouldn't drink your tea when it's still that hot. You'll burn your throat.'

Unbelievable... thought Aiden.

Must have taken five minutes to polish it all off. Frustratingly, prior to the conclusion of the meal, Mum, who up to that moment had been watching on with some amusement, disappeared back off to the kitchen, so that when Aiden was finally ready to be shown the "thing", there was no-one to do the job. Burning with frustration, he rose and went to extract Mum from the kitchen, taking the spent plate and cutlery through in order to provide an excuse for the visit.

'Are you going to show me, now?'

'Yes, you've suffered enough!'

At this point, the telephone rang. The telephone was situated back in the front room on top of the chest of drawers, immediately adjacent to the old-fashioned looking, modern, digital radio. The ring could be clearly heard here in the kitchen. Mum raced back into the front room, Aiden following and cursing within his insides.

'Hello,' Mum mouthed the phrase, 'Just be a minute,' in Aiden's direction as she waited for a reply. Aiden doubted this commitment, having witnessed many telephone conversations involving Mum on previous occasions.

'Oh, Hello, Janet. How are you?'

Aiden's heart sank. Mum turned the radio off... she was obviously intending to be in for the long haul. Janet was one of Mum's closest friends... she lived in a farmhouse higher up the valley, last house before you reached Dartmoor proper. This intermission could take a long time, yet more delay before she showed him the "thing".

'Yes, we have them here... Isn't it strange? Yes.'

Aiden could hear the voice of Janet but could not hear her words... could this conversation be linked to the mystery?

He suspected that it was.

'Must have come during the night... yes.'

Mum continued to look at Aiden throughout the exchange, making it all the more difficult for him to keep the cork in the bottle.

'No idea... no, I've not heard from anyone else, not yet... mind, it's still early.'

There followed a considerable delay as the tinny, indecipherable Janet-voice launched into a prolonged monologue. Mum nodded, an action considered by Aiden to be a waste of time. Plainly Janet couldn't see Mum nodding down the phone.

'Just about to show Aiden.'

At this, Mum smiled at Aiden, acknowledging his presence, Aiden responding with a grimace. Sounded as if whatever it was that Mum was going to show him (soon, please) was known to Janet... unlikely to be a bird then, Janet wasn't remotely interested in birds, very interested in talking, that was Janet, Aiden being unaware of any other hobbies in Janet's world. It suddenly occurred to Aiden that the mystery couldn't possibly be a bird in any case. No bird would be patient enough to wait this long to be introduced...and Mum would be fully aware of that.

Janet was broadcasting again, tinkling away as Mum nodded in response, occasionally looking straight at Aiden, occasionally saying 'yes' and then 'no.' The boy's attention began to drift and eyes to wander round the room. He glanced at Bobby in his cage, scraping his beak on the piece of cuttlefish bone, fixed to the bars for his delectation. The noise so produced seemed to merge seamlessly with the crackling sound of a distant telephone-bound Janet-voice to form a strange percussion, or a computer-generated sound effect.

Eyes then fell onto the china cabinet. The china cabinet was far too big for the room that housed it, took almost the entire length of the wall. Even if it had been half the size, it would still have looked out of place. Full of stuff it was, silver pieces and ornaments and cheap souvenirs from holidays and day trips. There was a little wooden object decorated with a picture of the seafront at Weston-Super-Mare, and a fossil of a trilobite that Mum had purchased from a shop in Lyme Regis, 'that will remind us of our visit...', she had said, '... whenever we look at this, we will remember this trip to Lyme Regis... I'll put it in the china cabinet when we get home.'

And that she did, and there it was.

Between the trilobite and a piece of agate, picked up from another shop, this one in Totnes, was a photograph in a plain wooden frame. Staring out from the picture, now and for all time, was the fresh-face of a young boy, younger than Aiden was now.

This was a photograph of Simon.

Simon had been Aiden's older brother but wasn't any more.

Simon had died some time ago, very suddenly and unexpectedly... some sudden illness, very unusual in a young boy, but these things occasionally happen.

Aiden just about remembered Simon but only just. He could remember playing football in the garden of the old house with Simon, the occasion when Simon had kicked the ball straight at him, and it had hit him square in the face, and he had cried a little bit. Dad and Simon had laughed at him, but when Dad realised that the ball had actually hurt him, he had walked across and comforted him, as best he could... though Dad wasn't very good at that sort of thing. Then Simon had started crying even though he was older... and hadn't been hurt at all... because he felt bad about hurting his little brother and because he thought he was going to be told off for doing it. Odd how that event had stuck in his mind, and so many others hadn't.

Aiden stared at the photograph of Simon as Mum continued to nod in response to the interference emanating from Janet at the far end of the line. The image in the china cabinet didn't really connect with the memory that he had of Simon because he couldn't actually remember what Simon looked like. The picture was all he had to go on, appearance-wise... very light brown hair and blue eyes, wide smile, but that would be because he was following orders from the photographer. Maybe he didn't really used to smile like that, except when following orders. When would it have been taken, this photograph of dead Simon? Aiden knew not... didn't even know how old Simon was in the picture, but it must have been taken not too long before he had died. Maybe it had been taken when he, Aiden, was five or six, or maybe when he had been a bit younger. Problem was, Simon's death was never mentioned these days, despite the photograph. The photograph was all that was left of Simon; there were now no words for Simon. He couldn't remember the death of Simon. After all, he had been quite young when it had all happened, and his brain had been very scrambled and was maybe trying to protect him from remembering. His memory was stopping him from remembering because if he did, it would be very frightening.

Dad had gone soon after Simon. There were no photo-graphs of Dad in the house.

'I've got to go now, Janet... yes, well goodbye then...'

Dad had just left, simply left. Again, Aiden couldn't remember exactly when, but it must have been soon after Simon had died. Memories were all very hazy as he looked at the smiling face of the youngster, staring out at him from the china cabinet.

He did remember waking up one morning, long time ago, with the sun roaring in through the window of his bedroom and feeling rather off-colour, not like he usually felt after waking up, feeling like something was not right without actually knowing why. This anxiety had led him to get out of bed rather quickly and to go downstairs, rather quickly. Mum was sitting alone in the front room crying, head sunk into her chest. Mum was really crying on that morning. He, Aiden, had no idea what to do, and so he just walked across the room to stand by Mum, stood so close that their bodies nearly touched. Mum didn't appear to notice.

'I've really got to go now, Janet, yes, really... no, goodbye!'

Dad was nowhere to be seen.

'Where's Dad?' Aiden had asked because he didn't know what else to say.

Mum didn't answer. Mum just kept crying.

It must have been ten or fifteen minutes, with Aiden standing so close to her that they were almost touching before she came round and told Aiden what had happened about Dad and how Dad had found Simon. Aiden listened but began to feel dizzy as the news sunk in, and so he had to sit down, then he had to cry too. Full story of Simon's death and what happened afterwards now emerged.

Seemed that Simon had been found by Dad in bed, dead, died in his sleep, killed by something that had happened overnight. After Mum had found out, Dad had gone for a walk to clear his head. Mum had wanted to call a doctor, but Dad had said that there was no point... it was too late. Mum had insisted that they call somebody... but Dad had repeated that there was no point, and then Dad had gone out.

Later that day Dad left the house again, this time for good as it turned out. Mum did not know that he was gone for good immediately but found out soon afterwards, maybe just a couple of days later, somehow. She had told Aiden late one afternoon, just after he had returned from school.

'Dad has left us for a while.'

'Why?'

'He is very upset over... what happened to... your brother. He needs time to think things through... please try not to be upset.'

Aiden was upset because he had loved Dad, and so he cried again.

'When will he come home?'

'Quite soon... as soon as he is able to.'

It must have been a week or so later when Aiden had asked the question again.

'When will he come home... Where is he?'

'He's fine.'

'Have you seen him? Where is he?'

'We've... spoken, he's fine.'

'Can I meet up with him... even if it's not here... I want to see him. I miss him.'

'He's... not able to meet you just now, Aiden... but he has told me to tell you that he loves you very much, and he will see you very soon.'

Aiden had kept asking the same question.

'When will he come home?'

Over and over and over again.

'When will Dad come home?'

'Soon, very soon.'

But he had not come home.

More than a month went by before Aiden stopped asking the question.

Despite the fact that there were no photographs of Dad in the house, at least, none that Aiden had seen, he was sure that he would recognise his Dad if he were to meet him again, just knew that he would.

'Can you smell something, Aiden?'

Aiden was lost in the photograph in the china cabinet and hadn't realised that Mum had finally escaped from Janet's phone call. Her question sort of drifted into his head, only becoming clear to him on the word, 'Aiden.'

'What... er sorry?'

'Can't you smell it, surely you can?'

There was some sense of stress in Mum's words, the emotion telegraphed to Aiden by a slightly elevated volume and a slightly higher pitch of the voice. A stranger may not have noticed it, but Aiden, having heard his Mum utter thousands, maybe millions of words, was sensitive to situations that weren't quite right... like this one. He was so wrapped up in the notion of something being not quite right in the tone of her voice that he quite neglected to note the actual subject of the question, so she had to repeat it again... almost angry this time. Then Aiden got it, and he could smell something, couldn't work out what it was, or what to call the smell, but it wasn't the usual front room smell.

'Mmm, yes, it does smell a bit funny...', looking at the birdcage and at Bobby looking back at him, he decided to proffer a possible cause, '... maybe it's the bird?'

Mum knew that it wasn't the bird.

'No, it's not that.'

Then she went to stand in front of the window... to look out into the garden, maybe the smell was coming from outside. Head swung to the right and left, almost seemed that she knew what she was looking for.

'What do you think it is?' Asked Aiden, Mum retreated from the window and was now standing in the middle of the room, rubbing the side of her face with her right hand.

'I think it smells like petrol,' said Mum convincingly.

Ah, thought Aiden, that could well be it... but in the front room?

'I know exactly what you mean... it does smell like petrol... it smells like a... garage... where you go to get petrol,' he added unnecessarily. Then he reflected that this had been an odd statement to make, as they, the family, he and Mum, didn't have a car, and therefore had no need to go to a garage to get petrol. Then, logic kicked in rapidly. These days, you didn't just buy petrol at garages, you bought all kinds of other things as well... so he would know what it smelled like to stand on a garage forecourt, even if he hadn't gone there to buy petrol. He remembered visiting a garage, not the details, but he had definitely been to a garage, so that would explain why he knew what a garage smelled like. That must be it.

Mum now stood stock-still in the middle of the room, Aiden now very anxious that there might be something very wrong with her.

'Are you OK?'

'Yes!'

That didn't help.

Mum read the signs and tried to calm things down.

'Yes, I'm fine, Aiden... nothing to worry about. You have to be careful with strange smells, better safe than sorry.'

Aiden smiled at this, and Mum smiled back at him. Bobby then decided that the angst had continued for far too long, breaking the silence with a ferocious bout of chirping.

'I'll swing for that creature,' Mum vowed as Aiden suddenly remembered the mystery thing that she was to show him.

'Weren't you about to show me something?'

Mum displayed a second of confusion before the brain rebooted, and the smile came back. This time it was a proper smile.

'Ah, yes, come on... it's outside.'

Aiden followed Mum out of the front room into the hallway and then to the front door... huge grandfather clock sounding out the seconds, very adjacent. The mysterious petrol smell hadn't made it out to the hallway... or maybe it had simply gone away. Door was opened into the garden. There was a low step from the hallway to the outside.

'Look, it's been snowing!' Said Mum.

Snow came to this corner of Devon most winters. After all, they were on the edge of Dartmoor; he and Mum had seen plenty of snow down the years. This had been quite a fall. The wall at the end of the garden boasted a thick, white crest, precariously perched on the narrow ridge of granite blocks. Garden itself was submerged, rose bushes nestling in the plot to the right of the path, and the hedge that bordered the next-door place, all covered, as was the lilac. The ash trees that grew beyond the garden, on the other side of the lane, might have featured in a Christmas card or a fairy story.

Aiden looked skywards, into a blue pool... the clouds that had brought the white stuff long since departed. The cold winter sun, still low in the sky, made the white land glare extra bright. The boy was so taken with the views across the lane and heavenwards and everywhere else that he failed to see that which Mum had wanted to show him.

'Look down, look at the path.'

There was a path that led from the front door to a gate that gave access to the lane. Aiden had not paid any attention to the path until Mum told him to. Now he did. Couldn't help but jump back.

'What made those?'

'Not sure.'

They both stared at the path, that section of path next to the front door of the house... and at the prints. The ground was snow-covered , except for those few inches that were closest to the door and thus benefitting from the heat emanating from within the hallway. The snow was about two inches deep on the main body of the path, and the prints went all the way down so that you could see the grey concrete beneath. Each print was maybe four inches long and three inches wide, being some eighteen inches apart and leading all the way up the path to the garden gate. The first print lay about twelve inches from the front doorstep of the house. Aiden had seen many footprints... and animal prints while out walking in the country, some in the snow and some on sand and some on the brown earth. In his judgement these looked a little like those of a cow.

'They look like a cows' prints,' he said to Mum.

'But they come out of the house... see, the first print is a footstep away from the house, when was the last time that you saw a cow walk out of our house?'

Aiden thought this statement to be false logic... even a sixteen-year-old could see the flaws here.

'But only you and me live in the house... and neither of us makes these kinds of prints.'

The prints were the mark of a cloven hoof, a two-toed foot, and they seemed to Aiden to be peculiarly well-defined, extremely stark. Not only did they go all the way down to the concrete of the path, but the edges of the prints also appeared kind of vertical, like a pie pastry sculpted with a cake-cutter.

'It's a real mystery, true enough,' said Mum.

'Maybe it is a small animal...', began Aiden, unconvincingly, then his thinking took off, and he continued excitedly, '... that happened to be just in front of the door when the snow started, and then, after a bit, headed off down the path, and made the prints.'

'What animal are you thinking of? These are cloven hoof-prints. What small animal has cloven hooves?'

'Maybe they were made by a bird.'

'Look at the size of them... if they were made by a bird, it must be an ostrich.'

'Ostriches do have two toes, though,' Aiden replied, but he was running out of steam, and Mum knew it. She did not respond but did point out another strange fact that Aiden hadn't appreciated.

'And they are in single file.'

Aiden tracked the prints with his eyes again, up to the garden gate... they did indeed lay in single file, almost... being displaced by merely an inch, right to left, as they progressed.

'Jesus, you're right... where do they go from here?' From where Aiden stood, the tracks stopped at the gate, but somehow, he doubted that that was really the end of them.

'I had a walk out earlier while you were still in bed, and they turn right at the gate and head up the lane towards Janet's.'

'That was the phone call from earlier?'

'Yep, they go past her farmhouse and continue up toward the moor.'

Aiden set off down the path, hopping from right to left to avoid the tracks. He just felt that he shouldn't tread on them.

'Where are you going?'

'To see where they go.'

Before Mum could pull him back, he was halfway to the gate, she shouted after him.

'You should put a coat on. It's cold.'

'I'm not going far, back in ten minutes.'

The plan was never to be executed, however. As Aiden neared the gate, he looked up the lane to the right in anticipation of a hunt for the trail of prints... and saw a familiar figure heading in his direction.

'Oh no... it's Mrs Youse!'

Mrs Youse lived alone (she had been married once, but the husband had died years ago), just up the lane from their house, on the way to Janet's place, but much closer to them than to Janet. She was very old, in her seventies, and more than a bit strange. Aiden had visited her house several times, often when delivering things. These visits had been necessary when Mrs Youse was unable to get out of her house... she had a bad leg and walked with the aid of a stick, but occasionally, the stick did not do the trick, and so she had to stay at home. It was then that Mrs Youse would phone Mum to ask her to buy milk and/or bread and/or other stuff from the village shop, and then Mum would ask Aiden to go to the shop and take the goods to Mrs Youse's house. The house was filthy and smelled very bad, and Aiden hated going there, but went there anyway, just for Mum.

Here was Mrs Youse coming down the path, God-fearing Mrs Youse, walking stick in the right hand, thrust repeatedly into the snow, tall, in a tatty old grey coat and a pink hat that seemed to be too large for her shrivelled head. As she came closer, Aiden could see more clearly her long white face and thin nose, and thin lips. Closer still and there was the brown spot on her left cheek with hairs growing out of it, and the dull, blank eyes and strands of grey hair poking out from under the incongruous, pink hat. As Aiden watched the figure approach, a crow perching proudly on a lilac branch at the edge of the next-door neighbour's garden, suddenly 'chacked' away into the sky. Aiden watched the creature fly away and wished that he could do the same.

The boy's attention was now divided, one part observing the old woman shambling towards him, the other noting the mysterious tracks walking, toes first, past Mrs Youse, up the hill towards Janet's place, just like Mum had said. The lane was pretty straight. Aiden could see half a mile or so up the hill before the road veered slightly to the right... long before that, the footprints... or hoof-prints had become impossible to pick out from the general white. Nevertheless, he couldn't prevent himself from staring, almost squinting to identify out the dark traces as they faded into the far distance.

'Hello, Aiden.'

'Hello, Mrs Youse.'

'Where's your mother?'

Aiden pointed to where Mum stood, still, at the door to the house.

'Ah, good!'

Mrs Youse paid him no further attention. Instead, opening the gate with a gloved right hand (walking stick temporarily transferred to the left) and then pushing past (there wasn't really room on the path for two, side-by-side), she headed for Mum. Aiden followed, distinctly hearing the old lady whisper the phrase, 'Jesus, they go to her front door.'

'Alice, Alice, what do you make of this then, eh?' Mrs Youse seemed more excited than was usually the case in Aiden's experience, 'Have you ever seen anything like this, eh?'

The tones were purest Devonian, vowels longer than your arm.

'What do you mean, Mrs Youse?'

Even Aiden, a sixteen-year-old, could see that Mum was being mischievous. Mum knew exactly what Mrs Youse was referring to.

'Whaat, whaat...?'

Mrs Youse had stopped halfway to the front door.

'... Well, this, of course!'

Mrs Youse jabbed her stick down, using it as a pointer, hovering above the nearest hoof-print, but not actually touching it.

'Ah... yes, strange, aren't they?'

'Strange isn't the start of it... they go right past my gate, right past... and then up the road towards Janet Drebbin's farmhouse.'

'Do they?' Asked Mum.

Mrs Youse stared directly at the front door of the house and acted as if she was about to say something but didn't seem able to do so ... eventually, following the passage of what seemed like ages, the dam broke.

'And they go to your front door!'

'So they do.'

'So, it must have come out of your house!'

'What do you mean by "it"?'

'Well, I'm not sure, but...', Mrs Youse gazed at the prints by her feet, eyes very wide, '... looks like the cloven hoof to me, or if not that, something very like it?'

'Looks like a hoof-print, sure enough.'

Mrs Youse appeared disappointed at this response. She thought that she knew what made the prints but didn't seem very keen on actually saying it. She would much rather someone else actually *said* it. Aiden had no idea what Mrs Youse was thinking but Mum did. She knew Mrs Youse well enough, she had heard the stories about Mrs Youse... and she was minded to force Mrs Youse to speak her mind... very mischievous.

'You've lived here a lot longer than me and Aiden...', she prompted, '... You've seen far more of this kind of thing than we have... What do you think has made the prints?'

'Well, this will sound strange to you... as you say, you not having lived round here as long as I have, but we in the country might see a set of prints like these, cloven hoof-prints you understand, and think that maybe we have been visited by a particular... creature, during the night.'

'We have been visited, Mrs Youse, that is plain to see, but by what?'

'Why... it seems to me that some... creature may have come in the night... some... thing... Satan... it's all in the Good Book, you know?'

Mrs Youse knew her Bible very well, studied it every Thursday night at eight o'clock until nine o'clock, at St. Michael's... her local church, led by the vicar, the Reverend Stapleton, fine man, the Reverend... very young for a vicar, but a fine man nevertheless. Mrs Youse knew her Bible very well and was almost certain that there was, in fact, no mention in there of Satan leaving tracks like these ones that led to the door of Alice's house, no cloven hoof-prints in the Good Book she was almost sure. She couldn't resist the "white-lie", though, not on this occasion... no chance that these two would know any different, probably these two had never opened a Bible at all.

'Now, now Mrs Youse...,' said Mum, in vindication, having known what Mrs Youse was eventually going to say, 'Is this you just having your bit of fun?'

Mrs Youse imported an especially serious expression to make it absolutely clear that she was not merely having her 'bit of fun'.

'Not at all, and you may well laugh...' (neither Mum nor Aiden were laughing), '... But what else could it be?'

'A cow?' Said Aiden.

'Can't have a cow coming out of your house, my boy... use your eyes, the prints are definitely coming out of your house. You don't keep cows in your house, do you, lad?'

'Don't keep devils either,' replied Aiden.

'Aiden!' Said Mum sternly.

The very serious expression, previously applied to Mrs Youse's face, was now replaced by one of lost hope.

'I'd better go... I've got some shopping to do.'

With that, Mrs Youse about-turned and marched with swinging stick, back up the garden path, followed by two pairs of eyes. At the gate, she looked round one final time before heading off down the hill, towards the centre of the village.

'What's the time, Aiden? I've not put my watch on today.' Mum asked.

Aiden glanced at his wrist.

'It's half-eleven.'

'My word... Aiden, could you do me a favour... could you pop down to the shop and get some bread and milk?... We're a little low.'

'Of course.'

'Walk slowly, or you might catch up with Mrs Youse... here's some money.'

Mum gave Aiden a hug.

Aiden returned to the house to pick up a coat whilst also soaking up some valuable time to allow Mrs Youse to pull well-ahead on the journey to the village shop. There was only one village shop, and so the two were bound for the same destination. Walked very slowly, she did, and so she would require a serious head-start to prevent the fast-walking Aiden from catching her up. Mum, standing outside the front door of their house, waved farewell to her son as he eventually exited the gate and turned left, sun still out and shining from a cloudless sky. Following the snowfall, the weather had been captured by one of those very settled spells that, in winter, makes blue sky and unbroken sun during the day and starry clarity at night. Aiden looked down at the snow-covered pavement of Flash Lane. There were no two-toed prints to see here. Unbroken snowy surface untouched by any animal, human or otherwise. Glancing behind as he walked along, Aiden now appreciated just how different the mystery-marks were, compared to his own trail, not just the shape, but also the... clarity... back to this "burned in" appearance, maybe made by a hot-iron and then Aiden stopped that thought because it was sinking dangerously close to the diagnosis that had been made by Mrs Youse, and he could see her fifty or more yards ahead... Was she really still so close? How slow could a human being walk?

Had to slow down.

He looked across the lane to his right, the parade of ash trees was still there, keeping pace with the young walker, but soon they would stop, and he would be able to see the river, the river Flash... or as the locals knew it, simply "The Flash".

The Flash made the name of the village... "Flashcombe", and of the lane. To confirm the point, he now passed the sign atop a post that was not quite vertical.

"WELCOME TO FLASHCOMBE".

"PLEASE DRIVE CAREFULLY".

You had to... the surface of the lane was so hostile, any attempt at high-speed travel would most certainly result in damage to any vehicle that was not a tank.

Mrs Youse crawled on ahead, nearly there, nearly at the village square, and in the village square was the shop. Both he and Mrs Youse were going to the shop. This was going to be a problem. Aiden decided to cross the lane just at the end of the parade of ash trees, to waste some time. On reaching the other side, he scrambled down the steep bank to reach the Flash, finding the river in a fiery mood. There had been a lot of rain over the past week, rain before the snow, soaking the moor, engorging the brooks and streams that fed the rivers, rivers like the Flash. Warm air had made the rain, but now it was cold, and so the snow had come, and with the snow had come the tracks and trails and prints, signatures of creatures large and small, human and otherwise.

The Flash and the boy made their way towards the village, the boy along the rough path, the water through its channel, brothers in arms on a freezing December day. Despite the weather, the Flash hadn't frozen over. It never did, never on the coldest of cold days, too much energy in the water, too much power to be overcome by ice, always kept running, always the same background song. Aiden couldn't recall the Flash ever freezing over.

A robin watched the world, atop a stone protruding from the mini-torrent. Time to get the phone out and take a photograph. Mum would love that, love a picture of a robin in mid-stream. Across the river were the playing fields of Aiden's school, empty today, all perfectly white... beyond the fields, he could see the low-slung school buildings, brooding and lonely in the holidays, waiting for the children to return. At his feet, the river, fresh from birth on the moors behind the village, rumbled cheerfully on, colour hard to define except for the occasional white plume as the water hit a troublesome rock. The banks were all rough grass and reeds at this point, with the occasional bush hanging tight, seemingly about to fall in, but never actually doing so. On several previous walks, Aiden and his mother had spotted water voles here, or maybe it was always the same one, no vole today though, this was no weather for a vole to be out in.

After walking for maybe ten minutes, with some difficulty as the path surface sloped alarmingly down towards the river at times, Aiden chose to negotiate the precipice to his left and re-join Flash Lane. The village shop was now in view, on the far side of the tiny square, nestling inconspicuously within a row of nineteenth-century cottages. To the right, the church, so beloved by Mrs Youse, stood behind a cloak of pines, within a sea of graves, all submerged in snow. On the roadside to the left, detached, isolated, and defiant, the pub, the "Moorland Huntsman", not at all beloved by Mrs Youse.

'Hi, Aiden. What are you up to!'

Aiden rose on his heels, apart from Mrs Youse, this was the first human contact yet experienced on the mission, Mrs Youse would be in the shop now, talking to Jenny, no-doubt informing on the devilish cloven hoof-prints that led from the Sweet house, this human contact was more to his taste. Helen came across from where she had been standing on the snowy island in the middle of the square, underneath a vast oak and next to the bench dedicated to a soldier that had been killed in World War One... Aiden couldn't remember his name, but he had lived in the village before he got killed.

Helen was a classmate and a friend.

'Hello, Helen.'

'Well, well, what's this all about, Aiden. What's this stuff about the Devil's Footprints?'

Aiden's heart sank.

'What have you heard?'

'Just that there are some weird tracks in your garden, and that...'

'Who told you?'

'Can't remember.'

'Yes, you can, someone must have told you... unless you have them in your garden... Do you have them in your garden?'

'No.'

'And have you actually seen them?'

'No... So you do have the tracks in your garden, then?'

Aiden realised that he was losing his temper. This was most unusual. He never lost his temper.

'Who told you, you must remember.'

'Nope... no idea.'

Aiden's assessment of Helen as a friend was up for reappraisal.

'Yes, you can, you must... Who told you?' Aiden stood very close to Helen, not in a deliberate attempt to intimidate. Aiden would never do that, even in his agitated state. He was, however, taller than Helen, so maybe he was being intimidating without meaning to be. Helen was sort of average to look at in the face, a bit like Aiden himself. The most notable thing about her was her hair (a riot of ginger curls) that always seemed to Aiden to have a life of its own, that did its own thing... not connected to Helen's brain, or maybe the hair had its own brain, a ganglion, like the big dinosaurs had, to control limbs that were too far away from their real brains to communicate.

'No, I can't remember. Maybe it was in a dream,' Helen replied, lying, obviously.

'Was it that old bat... Mrs Youse?'

'I haven't seen Mrs Youse in ages.'

'She's in the shop now... How long have you been here? You must have seen Mrs Youse going into the shop, so that's another lie.'

'You're mad. I'm ending this conversation now.'

That was that... true as her word, Helen not only stopped the conversation, she also ended the meeting. Before Aiden could react, she stalked off in the direction of her house on the lane next to the "Moorland Huntsman". Aiden had visited on a few occasions when they had been friends, big house it was, much bigger than his. Standing silently for several minutes, he watched the figure of Helen recede, suddenly feeling slightly ashamed and uneasy about the progress of events.

Then Mrs Youse emerged from the shop.

Aiden's reflective mood shattered. He looked for cover, didn't need to look far as he knew the square like the back of his hand. Ten yards to his left lay the haven of the bus shelter, Flashcombe being served by two buses a day, one at nine in the morning and one at two in the afternoon. The destination on both occasions was Hellstock, the nearest substantial town, set in the next valley. Currently, the shelter appealed to Aiden as a decent place in which to conceal himself from the demonic Mrs Youse.

The old woman shambled out of the shop and turned right, away from where Aiden was standing... looked like she was heading home... excellent. He could wait behind the concrete shelter until she disappeared out of view and then go into the shop to buy the bread and milk. The plan worked out to perfection, Mrs Youse heading away, away along the snowy path, an ever-decreasing threat, until she was gone, and so no threat at all. Aiden emerged from the bus shelter and jogged across to the shop.

'Hello, Aiden!'

'Hello, Jenny.'

Inside the shop it was dark, eyes needed to become familiar with the new light levels, and that would take a few seconds, therefore, he heard the voice of the shopkeeper almost before he could see her. Jenny wasn't *actually* the shopkeeper; she was the daughter of the shopkeeper. Jenny was in her fifties, slim, hair still holding on to brown, just. Kind of a sad face in profile, Aiden had always perceived her lips to be extremely thin, hardly any lips at all to speak of. Jenny's Dad owned the place... he was very old, and lived alone, next door to the shop. Aiden couldn't remember the last time that he had seen him; he was sick and rarely came outdoors. Jenny was married and lived with her husband in the village, fifteen minutes' walk away from the shop.

'How's your Dad?'

'Very kind of you to ask, Aiden. He's doing fine, just fine.'

'Good.' Aiden suspected that this wasn't entirely correct... folk often replied in this way because it was simpler than telling the truth.

'Aiden?'

'Yes...,' Aiden thought that Jenny was about to ask him what he wanted to buy, and he started to say, '... Bread.' Bread was behind the counter, a long counter stretching the full length of the shop, old-fashioned kind of shop. Also behind the counter were cakes and fruit and vegetables and that kind of thing, and medicines, only pills for indigestion and headaches and colds, nothing more than that. Behind Aiden, as he faced Jenny, guarding her long counter, were other daily consumables, lined on shelves... cans of things, packets of whatever, bottles of non-alcoholic-drinks.

Then Jenny said, 'What are these strange tracks in your garden that I've been hearing about?'

'I don't know what you mean.'

'Everyone's talking about it, y'know.'

'You mean Mrs Youse is talking about it.'

Jenny's mouth set into a thin line. What lips there once were had now gone entirely, 'What can I get you?'

'A loaf of bread, please.'

'Usual?'

Aiden nodded. He didn't know what type of bread was required, so was content to let Jenny decide. She turned and plucked a loaf from off a rack. She knew what kind of bread that Aiden's mum always bought, made it simple.

'Anything else?'

'A pint of milk, I'll get that myself', Aiden himself turned and made his way to an ancient fridge set against a wall... the profound effort expended in order to cool its contents sounded to Aiden like a cry of agony, a whispering scream.

'That it?'

'Yes.'

'One-fifty, please.'

Aiden handed over the money, producing the correct change.

'When did you first see 'em... these tracks?'

'Not sure... see you later, Jenny.'

Aiden felt very defensive about the hoof-prints, every question being taken as a personal attack... as if they were *his* fault. Maybe Jenny and Helen and all the rest of them thought that he had made the damned things, somehow... maybe they thought that he was the devil.

As he crossed the square, old Mr Jamieson who lived in the Tower House, shouted across to him. He was standing right outside the "Moorland Huntsman".

'Morning, Aiden... I've heard some strange tale about footprints in your garden. What's that all about, eh?'

Aiden pretended not to hear and walked quickly up Flash

Lane, heading for home and the strange tracks in the snow.

On the way back, an insane notion began to gnaw away, a revisit of the earlier thought, the one that had been displaced by the appearance of Mrs Youse, coming down the lane.

'It would be really interesting to find out where the footprints led.' It whispered.

'How could he find out where the footprints truly ended?'

'Easy, just follow them... just walk out of the garden, through the gate, and turn right up the hill.'

Aiden decided, there and then, that he would do just this. He would walk out of the garden, through the gate, and turn right up the hill, and he would, therefore, find out where the footprints truly ended. He considered the matter further as he walked home.

There followed an internal conversation between the voices of despair and common sense.

'What if you can't find the end?... What if you walk for days and days, through the woods and fields, across the moor, up and down again... and they just keep going, keep dragging you on, past the next tree, over the next bridge, and there they still are, stretching off into the distance? What if they go on forever?'

There came a reply from "common sense".

'Footprints, or hoof-prints, or animal-tracks can't go on forever. They must stop somewhere.'

'So, if they do stop, how do they stop? Will the marks just end, in the middle of a field... or on a riverbank, or at a wall?'

'That's silly. Tracks don't just stop.'

'So, they don't go on forever, and they don't just stop? What's left?'

The voice of common sense fell silent for the rest of the walk home. As Aiden approached the house, long before he reached it, he could see the black marks in the snow, still there, coming down the hill towards him.

Just in time for lunch, a sandwich would do.

'Are you sure that will be enough?' Mum had enquired, following the request.

'Yes, that will be fine.'

'What are you going to do this afternoon?'

'Haven't really thought about it.'

'Fair enough, you are on holiday after all.'

After lunch, Aiden decided to go out into the back garden. From inside the house, access was through the room-that-couldn't-really-be-used-for-anything behind the kitchen, there being a door set into the far wall that led to the outside. The back garden was half-lawn (under snow now, of course) and half allotment (also under snow). In the allotment half, they (largely Mum) would grow potatoes, peas, carrots, etc., far too many in most years, in most years much of the produce was distributed to neighbours and friends, Mrs Hills or Mrs Youse, or Helen's family. Aiden had tried to persuade Mum to set up a stall in the front garden where they could sell stuff.

'That's silly, Aiden, no-one ever comes past our house.'

Now Aiden could say, if he so wished, 'Maybe the devil comes past our house... maybe he comes *inside* our house... we could sell our potatoes to him!' As he walked out into the back garden, the boy couldn't help but smile at the image of Satan stopping at their stall out the front and buying a bag of potatoes from Mum.

At the very back of the back garden was the shed. Behind the shed was the back-garden fence, and behind this, a field. This field belonged to the Miles' farm, but Aiden could not remember any of the Miles family (there were two sons and a daughter to Richard and Sarah, all of them "employed" to work on the farm), or any of the farm-hands ever being spotted in this field. Maybe they didn't need it any more, for whatever reason, though someone must be looking after it as it wasn't overgrown.

The shed had been there forever, a stout, wooded box, very square, with a flat roof and a curious window that faced Aiden as he approached. Odd to have a window in a tiny shed, he had always considered, but there it was, dark glass reflecting the dark inside. A concrete path, crunchy white now, took him to the right of the shed and to the door which he opened (it was never locked), and then he was inside. Inside was about twenty feet by twenty feet, window to the left above a bench with various tools scattered on its surface. These tools must have belonged to Dad, even though both he and Mum now used them as if they were their own. A rake, hoe, and shovel leaned against the opposite wall, grouped round a bucket, and next to that congregation, an old, battered stool, a perch that Aiden loved to sit on, by himself, and think about life. The stool wasn't especially comfortable, but that property kept the user awake and alert, therefore promoting deep contemplation.

It was quite light in the shed, maybe the window had been a good idea after all... although the inside of the place appeared dark from the outside, that wasn't the case when you actually stood or sat on the stool inside. Aiden now seated himself on the stool and worked up his plan to discover where the footprints truly ended. Deciding that he would set off on the next weekend, he earmarked the route to be... out of the garden, then turn right up the hill, and just keep walking until the prints stopped. If he went on Saturday, there would be ample opportunity meantime to formulate detailed plans.

Later in the afternoon, after Aiden had returned to the house, news arrived which would change everything. Mum was watching TV as he entered the front room, the local evening news programme was on, and at the very moment of Aiden's entry, the news presenter, sitting behind her desk on the screen, passed over to the weather presenter, standing before his weather map.

'Good Evening,' said the young weather presenter from the TV, 'You'll be pleased to know that this current very cold spell is coming to an end. If you have snow in your garden today, I can promise that it will all be gone by Wednesday.'

'Good job too!' Said Mum.

'But if the snow melts, we'll lose the footprints!'

'So what?'

'But I want to know where the footprints end.'

Mum shrugged her shoulders and looked back at the TV screen, 'Nothing I can do about that,' but she then added, 'the forecast says that it will warm up by Wednesday... you still have tomorrow.' Aiden smiled, Mum smiled back. She would also quite like to know where the footprints ended, merely out of curiosity.

'I could go out tomorrow, tomorrow, after lunch.'

'Why not? You are on holiday after all.'

Mum left for the kitchen with Aiden watching the rest of the TV weather forecast, 'The outlook for next week is for a warmer spell... warm air from the South is expected to spread throughout the country by the middle of the week.' Aiden wasn't much concerned about the middle of next week, mind busily turning to the expedition which would now definitely take place tomorrow. Mum returned presently, at the same time as the weather presenter handed back to the news presenter, 'And here are the main headlines at...', news presenter looked away from the camera for a moment, '... just after five-thirty...'

Following dinner (cottage pie), Aiden climbed the stairs, thoughtfully, to his room. There hadn't been a great deal of conversation at the meal... Mum seemingly, preoccupied... Aiden himself was also preoccupied... with tomorrow. Now, within the sanctity of his own private place, sitting on the edge of the bed, he meticulously planned the search for the end of the footprints. He foresaw no significant problems, being sure, in his own mind, that he had all the tools necessary to do the job.

Walking boots and socks.

Rucksack.

Windproof jacket and trousers.

Sandwich box and plastic bottle in case of an emergency.

Whistle, again in case of emergency.

Compass, and the skill to use it properly.

Ordnance Survey map of "Flashcombe and Hellstock" at 1:25000 scale, surely the tracks wouldn't extend out of the area of "Flashcombe and Hellstock"?

All the above had been acquired to facilitate bird-watching trips with Mum but would be vital for the imminent expedition. Despite his confidence that the map of "Flashcombe and Hellstock" would include all possible sites of the termination of the footprints, he hadn't a clue how long his journey would be... this being the great unknowable. Though concerning for a short while, Aiden decided, in due course, that as this was an uncontrollable component of the trip, he should just ignore it, so he did.

Mind was full of the events to come, even as he got into bed. Doubted that he would be able to sleep but, after half-an-hour of white brain-noise that caused him to turn over several times, the clouds gathered, and he danced into the night.

Next morning welcomed with a glorious day, low sun beaming through the bedroom window... sky cloudless yet again, excellent weather for an adventure. Had a wash as usual and went down to breakfast... toast and marmalade again, eaten to the accompaniment of Bobby's provocations from the cage, and under the watchful gaze of Simon, looking on from within his photograph. Then it was time to gather the equipment together for the journey. As Mum cleared away the spent plates, Aiden rose, full of positive intent, and then...

... And then there was a knock on the door.

Mum, halfway to the kitchen, was forced to retrace her steps and deposit her cargo of spent plates and cutlery onto the table.

'That'll be Mrs Hills, with the books.'

Mrs Hills ran an informal book club in the village.

Mum headed for the front door.

Mrs Hills typically visited about once a month on book club business, sometimes she came more often than that, but the other times were just to gossip and drink tea.

'Hello, Veronica!' Mum's muffled voice leaked into the front room from the hallway. There followed a similarly muffled response:

'So, it's true about the tracks then... I'll be blowed, never seen nothin' like it... Have you ever seen anythin' like that, Alice, eh?'

'It's a mystery, Veronica. It truly is.'

By this time, the two women had made their way into the front room.

'Ah, Aiden is here, hello, Aiden!' Veronica Hills' voice rose by an octave as she saw the boy sitting at the acting dining table.

'Hello, Mrs Hills. How are you?' Aiden replied, the perfect young gentleman.

'Well, how very kind of you to ask, such a polite boy, eh... Alice?'

Mrs Hills was a substantial body of flesh, very square in appearance... square shoulders, prominent in her thick not-really-fur-but-looks-like-it-coat, short hair making her head look similarly symmetrical, even the nose was unusually angular, digitised, made not from a continuous wave but rather from distinct points, joined together with lines.

'Anyway, I have the books that you ordered last month, here we are...'

Mrs Hills unleashed a large carrier bag displaying a "Marks and Spencer" corporate logo and began to extract the requested items.

'... Hold on. This one isn't yours... ', a book was raised, an Olympic Torch for all to see, '... "Legends of Devon", that'll be for Mrs Youse, she's next on the list... though looking at what's in your garden, Alice, I reckon this book should have another chapter!' Mrs Hills thought this last remark hilarious, and laughed accordingly. Mum and Aiden smiled.

'Here are your books...', three more titles were unveiled, '... Do you know, Alice...' All of Mrs Hills' words were directed at Mum, '... I always remember everyone's books?... Don't need to make any notes... all up here.' Mrs Hills jabbed a finger to the side of her head in order to emphasise the power of her spectacular memory.

'"Birds of Britain"... Is this one for you, Aiden? "Agatha Christie", for you, Alice? And a biography of Winston Churchill... can't guess that one!'

The three books were deposited onto the table with a flourish. Aiden wanted to leave, desperately. He had work to do.'

'I'd better go and get my things together.'

'Things together, eh? Are you off somewhere, young Aiden?'

'Sort of, Mrs Hills.'

'Are you sure that you don't want to look at the book-list for next month?'

'I'll give it a miss, Mrs Hills.'

Aiden strode out of the front room with intent.

'Don't forget your "Birds" book!'

Aiden smiled impatiently, aborted his mission, and returned to pick up the book... it had a picture of a bittern on the front dustcover... Aiden recognised it immediately. He owned plenty of birds' books, of course, but was always open to new resources.

'Goodbye, Mrs Hills.'

Running up the stairs to safety, Aiden rapidly assessed the locations of the various bits and pieces that would be required... by the time he reached the top he believed that he pretty much knew where everything was. Walking boots and socks... easy... former in the bottom of the wardrobe, latter in the sock drawer. The windproof jacket and trouser set also lived in the wardrobe, hung up on coat hangers. Rucksack simply rested against the wall next to the wardrobe. The other items lurked inside a large but flat basket to be found under the bed, this being a kind of storage space for outdoor necessities, whistle, compass, maps, plastic bottle, and sandwich box, also walking guides to Dartmoor, binoculars (Aiden didn't intend to take the binoculars... they were old-fashioned and quite heavy... handy for bird-watching... but this trip would not be a bird-watching trip, and so he wouldn't take the binoculars, didn't need binoculars to see two-toed hoof-prints, at your feet).

In next to no time, everything was ready to go... and then he realised that the sandwich box and plastic bottle were both empty (of course they were), sandwiches and water being therefore required. Water was simple, available from the bathroom tap, but in order to acquire sandwiches (plus crisps, apple, etc.), he would have to go downstairs again. Might be better to wait until Mrs Hills had gone, it was still relatively early, and it had never been his intention to leave until the afternoon. Standing at the top of the stairs, Aiden could hear

Mrs Hills say her goodbyes to Mum. This usually took some time because Mrs Hills always had something extra to say just before she left.

'Oh... and by the way Alice, our Linda had a hell of a do at the doctor's last Thursday...' or,

'I should have told you, Gerald (Gerald was Mrs Hills' husband, he'd been quite ill recently, so Mum had told him, without giving any details) won a bit of money on the horses at the weekend... only ten pounds but better than nothing.'

However, as luck would have it, on this occasion, Mrs Hills was a little pressed for time.

'I'd love to chat, Alice, but I've got to go... we're getting a new cooker, and the man is due to come at eleven, and I still have to deliver to Mrs Youse... I'll see you later... Bye!' From his lofty perch, Aiden could monitor Mrs Hills' progress into the hall. Mum did not follow. Instead, calling from the front room.

'Goodbye, Veronica, thanks for the books!'

Mrs Hills let herself out.

Aiden raced down the stairs to make his sandwiches.

'Do you want some lunch before you go?' Enquired Mum, emerging from the front room.

Aiden was suddenly very keen to get on the road... he could make lots of sandwiches. Some would be for use in case of emergency... and the rest he could eat for lunch.

'Actually, Mum, I think I'll make some sandwiches, pack up and get going.'

'Are you sure you don't want to wait until after you've had lunch? Yesterday you said you would go after lunch.'

Mum didn't sound very pleased.

'Will that be OK?' Enquired Aiden.

It wasn't so much that Mum wasn't very pleased... it was more that she was quite worried. Yesterday when they had discussed the trip, Mum wasn't convinced that Aiden would actually do it. Teenagers came up with all sorts of crazy ideas... Grand Plans of what they may do... and rarely actually did them.

'I suppose so... make sure that you take all the proper things, proper boots, and your windproof jacket, all that kind of thing... and a map and a whis...'

So, it wasn't just a 'Why don't you wait until after lunch' thing. It sounded like a 'Do you think you should go at all' thing. Aiden chose to gloss over this, moving on to detail.

'I know, Mum, I've packed everything up... upstairs. I just need to make some sandwiches for lunch.'

'You should make more... just in case... and take your phone... just in case.'

That was stupid. Of course he would take his phone... but...

'I will, of course, but you know how bad the reception is higher up the valley... I may not be able to use it.'

Mum's face creased that bit more.

'How far do you think you will have to go?'

'No idea...'

The increasingly disturbed and disturbing expressions on Mum's face suggested that the last statement hadn't gone down well at all. Aiden picked up the vibes and decided to try and row back.

'... I'm sure that it can't be that far. If a small animal made the prints, it wouldn't get that far... and I may not get to the end of the trail anyway.'

Mum appeared to be slightly mollified by this.

'Just be careful... and keep an eye on your watch. If it starts to get late, just turn round and come back. You mustn't be away overnight.'

'I will,' Aiden tried a smile, but he was desperate to be off and still had to make his sandwiches.

'I should make my sandwiches.'

'Make sure that you come straight back if it gets too late...

I know what you're like.' Mum's turn to smile now, a smile from an affectionate, anxious and proud Mum. Aiden went in to the kitchen and ravaged the fridge for cheese and ham and salad things for his sandwiches. He also procured two bananas and an apple from the fruit basket on the vast, central table, then it was back upstairs to carry out final preparations. Downstairs, Mum looked out of the front window, just able to make out the tracks on the footpath... couldn't see them too clearly, from here they appeared as black stains on the dazzling white of snow, couldn't discern the strangeness from here.

Bobby, who had been sleeping, awoke as Aiden burst into the room, backpacked and ready to go. Consequently, the lad's entry was accompanied by a cacophony of chirps and whistles, an avian fanfare for the soon-to-depart.

Simon looked out from the past as Mum smiled at the other son.

'Make sure you come home before it gets too late.'

'I will.'

'Bye.'

'See you later. I'll be home before it gets dark.'

'Bloody right you will!'

Aiden about-turned and left the front room, under the gaze of Mum and the rioting Bobby and the dead Simon in the photograph.

Out into the hallway and out of the front door, accompanied by the chimes of the great clock in the hall, as Mum watched from the window. Aiden waved from the footpath, trying not to stand on the prints, executing a crazy dance, waving and hopping from one foot to another, both actions executed simultaneously.

First steps on the great adventure to discover where the tracks ended. First steps under a sky that continued to stand still, dazzling blue inside without a memory of cloud or wind, the weather-clock had stopped. To the end of the path, in his walking boots, wearing his windproof jacket and trousers, rucksack on his back containing the sandwich box (now containing sandwiches) and plastic bottle (now containing water).

The whistle was attached to his belt, and the map was in the large, left-breast pocket of the windproof jacket, and the compass was tied to the outside of the rucksack with a spare shoelace. A more well-equipped, young adventurer, there might never have been.

Mum was still watching from the window as Aiden exited through the gate, following but not disturbing the line of prints, racing ahead of him now, to the right, up the hill, leading him on, taking him to some conclusion yet to be elaborated. Past the next-door neighbours' place (the Hartsons lived there, nice old couple... Mr Hartson was a keen gardener, though you couldn't see many of the fruits of his labours today). There had been no fresh snow, but the fall from the weekend hadn't melted at all. Aiden bent down and touched the cold edge of a cloven-hoof track and then realised...

He had forgotten to bring gloves!

He could return to the house now... it wasn't too late... he was only just past the Hartsons' place. No, he would press on, he wasn't intending to be away from home for long... and the windproof jacket hosted deep pockets... he wasn't too keen on wearing gloves in any case.

The indentation of the tracks, so sharp, almost branded into the snow, fed yet more fantastical thoughts into the head of young Aiden, thoughts that muttered amongst themselves and then began to recall the words of Mrs Youse. Aiden told them all to be quiet so that he could concentrate on the matter in hand.

On the other side of the road, the Flash had meandered carelessly close to Flash Lane, no tree-screen to hide behind from now on... and as the gradient so slowly increased, the water, with increasing energy, sang ever louder, tumbling over granite boulders made on the moor, laid down on the riverbed in more violent times. On Aiden's side, there were two more houses to pass before Mrs Youse's house, and then civilisation gave way to open ground. The house before Mrs Youse's was occupied by Mr Echeway and was in a state of some disrepair... Mr Echeway was very old and lived on his own. He didn't go out much. A daughter came to visit once a week on Sunday afternoons, but other than that, Aiden knew little about him. On passing the house, he noted that all of Mr Echeway's curtains were drawn and that all the rooms behind the curtains appeared to be in darkness. A thought occurred that he might knock on Mr Echeway's door to check that he was OK... following a glance down at the path, snow-covered, and with the tracks ever-present, he decided against it. In any case, Mr Echeway, in addition to being old, and possibly because of it, was deaf, and therefore, he probably wouldn't hear the knock. Aiden walked on, almost ran past Mrs Youse's place in an attempt to avoid being spotted. Didn't want Mrs Youse opening the door and beckoning him over for a chat; he didn't have the time. Mrs Youse's garden was a total mess, just like the inside of her house, but on this day the snow disguised the state of the outside, at least. In a heartbeat he had left the houses behind and now stood at the edge of Flashcombe.

To the right, behind a wooden fence, lay a white field often occupied by horses but not today. There were fences, jumping fences, two of them, at opposite ends of the field, and a large pile of straw in the centre now, disguised as a pile of snow. The horses that weren't there were the property of the Mackinnon family who lived in a big house just past the church in the centre of the village... they must own the field as well, thought Aiden, as he walked past. On the other side of the lane, the river gurgled on, not too many big boulders in the riverbed at this point, and so the surge of the water was less dramatic; the noise now a whisper, rather than a shout, conversation more measured. One or two trees, ash, willow, a tall and elegantly out-of-place spruce, made a dismal attempt to shield the Flash from view, but there it was, clear as day, in its shallow channel, making its way home, up on the Moor.

Now a significant event, the paved footpath at the traveller's feet was about to stop. Due to the snow cover, there was no obvious visible change, but Aiden knew the truth, from countless previous trips. At this point in the journey, the concrete path became a dirt track... not that this made any difference in the current situation.

Ahead the route continued as a right-of-way that would host his boots, as it had hosted the creature that had come before, the creature that had made the prints. On they continued, along the line of the way, one after another, burnt into the snow. A battered fence now joined him as a companion as he strode on, on into the Scarecrow Field.

Scarecrow Field, so-called because, for many years, its owner, a local farmer whose name Aiden could not remember, maintained a scarecrow close to the stone wall that formed the rear boundary of the plot. At some time, some past time, this must have been a field of crops, hence the need for the scarecrow, but there were no crops here now, instead an overgrown mini-jungle of wild grasses, some poking above the snow cover, providing a startling relief from the blazing white landscape. No scarecrow now, but Aiden remembered it, it had been here until quite recently, and Aiden used to be quite scared of it when he was younger. The farmer, whose name he could not remember, had equipped the statue with a loathsome face, fangs for teeth, eyes that looked like real eyes, totally unnecessary of course, the birds would not be any more afraid of a hideous head than they would have been of any other... and Aiden hadn't known what the fangs or the eyes were made of that made them look so real, after all, he had been very young, then. The memory caused Aiden to accelerate in order to reach the end of the Scarecrow Field as quickly as he could. In passing, he looked at the spot where the cloth monster used to stand and paused for a moment, lost in his past. Now it was gone, and there was nothing to be afraid of.

Ahead, the ground began to rise again.

Ahead was Watchman's Wood.

Aiden's heart lifted; once he was through Watchman's Wood, he would be as good as on the Moor... surely the prints couldn't go on much further, once he was on the moor? Spirits boosted, and with the Flash at his side, chattering away, he pressed on. Suddenly, from the corner of his left eye, or so it seemed, he sensed movement. Initially he was unable to distinguish the direction from which it came, but following a little mental processing, he looked in what he assumed was a promising direction, about ten o'clock to the direction of travel (the direction of travel being twelve o'clock). There he saw a dog, a dog with a back of reddish hue... no, no dog, this was a fox, bright-eyed and ears erect, ambling along the back edge of the Scarecrow Field, hugging the wall forming the unnatural barrier with the woodland beyond. As Aiden stared at the animal it seemed to respond, looking back at the boy, meeting his gaze with pure defiance; who would blink first? He had seen many foxes over the years, hereabouts, on the fringes of the moor, and so this sighting did not surprise him unduly. Half a minute passed, and the fox lost interest in the presence of the human, diving off through a hole in the fence and into the wood.

Watchman's Wood.

The contrast was extraordinary.

One moment, Aiden was standing in the open country, beneath a blue ceiling, eye-jousting with a fox, the next he was immersed in the dark magic of another world, the old-oak landscape of a different age. This was a truly fantastical place, born from the pen of Tolkien, this Middle-Earth at the foot of the moor. Watchman's Wood, a mass of twisted trees, snakes in timber finding every imaginable, and unimaginable direction in which to grow. Bending this way and that, indirectly upwards only to meet yet more sinuous branches that blocked their path, the trunks deviating yet again, desperate to reach the sky. The web of branches made it dark inside... and it *was* inside, inside the wood as if inside a cave, a wood with a roof that had kept out the snow so that all of the unwhite life was there to see. Rumbling away somewhere, out of sight, but very much within hearing was the Flash, now secure in a deep channel and having to work very hard to find its way... the great tree-roots projecting out of the soil proving formidable obstacles.

What of the tracks?

There was no snow in the wood, no surface to hold the marks of the creature!

Aiden paused to take stock and then smiled with a kind of relief as he absorbed the scene before him.

No snow on the ground... but that which had become trapped at the top of the canopy had melted, the tops of the trees had made rain, and this had turned the soil to mud, soft mud preserved by cycles of freezing and thawing. So, the prints continued, not in white but in brown, forging forward up the crazy, eccentric path that dodged between the tree roots and monstrous undergrowth... same shape, same two-toe echo, same single-file style. Aiden followed the frozen mud trail, any snow that had clung valiantly on to the boots up to this point rapidly displaced. Progress demanded great application and effort, partly because the conditions underfoot were treacherous with precarious ledges and steep ridges that would twist an ankle if given a chance. More critical for the adventurer, however, was the state of the trail that he was determinedly following... this periodically becoming less distinct in patches where the mud had flowed, making the prints hazy and almost invisible. Aiden needed to concentrate very hard so as not to lose the scent.

Beneath his feet, the hill grew ever steeper, the trees to right and left increasingly twisted and now vaguely threatening with the clattering Flash out there somewhere and a tap-tap-tap of an invisible woodpecker, which, in this oddly hostile environment, was a source of comfort for Aiden. He looked around, up at the mangled wood, but there was no sign of the green burst of the bird itself.

And then he was out of it.

As swiftly as he had been submerged by the wood, he was now released from its ambiguous care into the snowy world outside, a world very different to that of the Scarecrow Field. Now he was really on the Moor, on the Common. Negotiation of a style was now required, achieved with practised ease. On the other side, the tracks resumed, back in snow, burned into the crust. A bird, possibly a thrush, had left tiny three-toed sketches alongside the hoof-prints.

The land continued inexorably on and up.

Aiden took in the drama ahead, nothing but a blanket of white...almost...a few boulders, scattered across the bleak hillside were still grey, oddly free of snow, but the monochrome was otherwise unrelenting. To the right, the ground dropped away, and Aiden could clearly see the Drebbins' farm, laying in a hollow beneath the swelling ridge, about half-a-mile away, smoke twirling up into the sky from a lone chimney. He considered paying them a swift visit, but time was not on his side. A look at his watch produced a curse; it was later than he thought... he would have to turn back in thirty minutes, forty-five tops, if he was to get home before dark...and he hadn't eaten lunch. Beyond the Drebbins' place, the shoulders of Dartmoor continued to expand, rolling waves of snow-covered surge, the presence of the snow making the view more sea-like than ever. To right and to left, the high ground began to impose itself, to take the eye up, ever-more rising to the tops, many crowned by rocky piles, granite exclamation marks, exuberant conclusions in stone and snow.

Aiden went on. Twenty yards to the right from where he stood, there emerged from the Moor a weather-beaten stone monolith, about as tall as he was... the Druid's Stone. Stationed majestically on top of the rising ground behind and above the Stone was the first summit of the Moor... H'ell Tor.

The Druid's Stone was as white as everything else in this arctic world, pale finger prodding up, pointing at a sky, while though still blue, was definitely feeling its age.

Aiden had done a 'project' on the Druid's Stone at School a while back. The teacher, Mrs Clerk, had tasked the class with composing an essay on a 'local landmark of choice'. Helen had chosen the village church, a subject that had seemed a little dull to Aiden.

'That's a bit boring,' Aiden had told her, rather cruelly.

Helen had scowled and attempted to get her own back by asking, 'Well, what have you chosen?'

'Druid's Stone.'

'That seems more boring to me.'

There the conversation had ended, for the time being.

Aiden had learned that the Druid's Stone wasn't actually a Druid's Stone, merely a medieval reminder of some land-boundary. The strange horizontal lines on the face of the thing, therefore, did not mark the cuts made by axes or knives in the act of severing peoples' heads as part of a service of sacrifice; though Mrs Clerk had not proffered an alternative explanation.

There was no path at all now, not even a dirt track, didn't change anything, of course, he would continue to walk on snow and would have to do the best he could from here on. Meanwhile, whatever, or whoever had made the trail that had brought him to this point, just kept on going, stretching out before him, a long line of black within the white, climbing the hill towards H'ell Tor. Aiden scrambled on... not much time now. The sky was telling him, urgently now, that the time was short to complete the mission. If the tracks continued beyond H'ell Tor he would simply have to turn back and admit defeat. This negative thought was quickly dismissed.

H'ell Tor.

A massive pile of granite blocks left exposed by millennia of erosion that had stripped away the surrounding rock. Aiden knew this place well, but he had never come here when the ground had been so white. It was almost a new place to him, a foreign land that should have been so familiar. Almost there now, almost at the top of the hill... from there he would be able to see beyond, to the next summit, Skip Tor, but he wouldn't be going to Skip Tor today. There was no time. This would be the end of the road, one way or another.

As he approached, H'ell Tor dominated the view ahead. On a summer's day, the rock would have appeared grey against the sky, weathered to dullness. Today, only a few slices of the bare granite could be seen, revealed by perching birds dislodging snow from the massive boulders. On the ground, the tracks bore down on the stones, aiming straight for the highest point of the hill, the certainty of the creature's progress continuing, even in this wilderness. Aiden reflected that, thus far, there had been no deviation, no false diversions, or seeming mistakes in the progress of the prints, relentlessly and remorselessly, their maker had continued on its journey. Maybe, they were destined to come here, this lonely pile of rocks always the intended termination.

Time to tread carefully, he knew what was coming. The Flash, content in its deep channel and chirping to the world on its journey up the hill, now swung sharply to the right. On a previous walk, maybe the first that had brought Aiden to this place, he had very nearly tumbled over close to this point, not anticipating the sudden appearance of the stream's trench. This time he was prepared, prepared for the Flash, but not for the behaviour of the tracks.

The tracks stopped on the brink of the stream's bank.

Initially, a glance to left and right gave no clues, the creature had not attempted to find a crossing. Instead, and this sight chilled Aiden to the bone... and his bones were already very cold... he could see that the prints recommenced their journey on the opposite bank, as if the Flash simply wasn't there.

Aiden stared.

This was kind of impossible.

But maybe not... maybe when the animal, or whatever it was, came through, the stream was frozen, and so it was able to walk across, ah... that would be it. But the Flash never froze; it flowed too quickly to freeze. Aiden could not remember the Flash freezing, ever...

The trough was about eight feet wide at this point, too far to try and jump across, for him at least, but there was no need because twenty feet upstream were the Flash Beads. Clearly, the creature had no need to make use of the Flash Beads. Aiden turned and followed the stream's bed on rising ground, and there were the Beads... stepping stones, maybe dropped to carry an old drover's route across the water. In this weather they would not be straightforward to negotiate, but there was no choice. The sky was starting to dim, no longer a dazzling blue, the pure colour appeared now mixed with a darker shade. God was mixing the pallet and time was moving on.

But safely across the Beads and the Tor was now so close...

and Aiden just knew that the prints would not go beyond the granite stones, and he would be able to go home and tell Mum that he had found out the source, if not what had made them. He wasn't sure that he really wanted to know what had made them.

Snow was very deep here, the winds blowing across the Moor's broad back had built vertiginous drifts. At one point he almost sank knee-deep into a powdery morass, but he kept going, up to the Tor... closest stones were now very close, just yards away. Breath was short and condensed in the cold air, making clouds invisible in the gloom.

Sky was darkening by the minute... for the first time, Aiden noted the pale crescent of moon, high in the sky... first tendrils of panic began to assail his brain. He absolutely needed to turn back the moment he reached H'ell Tor and found the source of the Devil's Footprints.

Now he was at the top where the ground levelled out into a series of hillocks and holes. Granite boulders sprang randomly, around and about, partially covered by snow, grey and white, stone holding bits and pieces of green vegetation, still surviving, despite winter's best efforts. The Flash, now much diminished, was losing its identity, demerging into a series of rivulets and springs, energy sapped by the low gradient.

Passing between the boulders while scrupulously following the two-pronged hoof-prints, Aiden reached the absolute summit. Beneath the fading sky, he couldn't help but waste time looking around. Ahead, maybe half-a-mile away, lay Skip Tor, a hundred feet or so higher than his present perch, but only reached by dropping into a deep combe and then regaining elevation... and then some more. There were more distant peaks. Aiden knew the names of some of them... Bell Tor, High Fourways, Clock Hill... but not all.

Mum smelled it again.

The same smell as before, in the same place as before, adding to the anxiety.

Aiden had not come back, and it would soon be dark.

She had tried to call her son, but there was no reply, no signal, just like Aiden had promised... he was such a bright boy.

That petrol smell again.

That smell that was always in the house when John came home from work. Aiden's Dad worked in a petrol station for a time and always came home smelling of petrol.

'Can't you clean yourself off before you come home?' Alice had exhorted.

'I do the best I can, but there's no shower at work, and no place to change,' Aiden's Dad had said. The other time that the petrol smell had flooded the house, she had assumed that it was just one of those things, because that was what she wanted it to be. This time, it couldn't really be one of those things again.

Aiden smelled it too, high on H'ell Tor, and he remembered it from the last time, the time when it had triggered an old memory that he could not properly recall. High, at the top of H'ell Tor, close to dusk, Aiden knew that he should be alone, but knew also that he wasn't. Tracks of the creature still there, taking his vision to the topmost stone, square and grey... light was fading fast, and so the white was grey now.

He should turn back.

A figure walked from out of the stone, twenty feet away. Maybe from behind the stone, couldn't be from out of it... that would be impossible. The man, it was definitely a man, looked to be tall, strong, and square-shouldered, too dark to make out any other features. Aiden stood stock still, filled by emotions that he would never be able to understand.

'Hello,' he shouted because he felt that he had to.

'Hello to you... a rotten day to be out, what on Earth has brought you out here?'

Aiden felt that the question could be reciprocated but chose to say nothing.

He was very cold now... it was almost dark. Had to turn back, but it may be too late... he might have to try and get to the Drebbins' farmhouse; that might be the best hope. Having this potential plan made him feel better as the figure, now clear of the highest stone, began to walk toward him.

And the petrol smell was almost overpowering; the sweetness of it made him feel sick. How could there be a petrol smell here, here in the middle of a frozen nowhere? Smelling petrol in the front room of a house was one thing, but how so here?

Mum realised that she needed to sit down in the front room.

Bobby was quiet in his cage, sedated by something unknown, clinging to his perch closer to death than to life.

The man that had come out from behind the granite screen had a very familiar shape, seemed to have the same shape as Dad, his Dad as was, all of those years ago. Aiden recognised the shape of him, here and now, always he knew that he would, even if he couldn't actually *picture* Dad in his head. Couldn't be Dad, though... impossible, but it was, it definitely was.

Still asked the question, though, had to.

'Who are you?'

'Don't kid on Aiden. You know who I am!'

Aiden wasn't especially surprised that the stone-man knew who he was,

'Where have you been... what happened to you?'

Words echoed round his head before exiting his mouth, phrase just building itself from somewhere deep... machine code, not comprehended by the user, made in the Aiden-brain.

'Never mind, main thing is that I am here now.'

Mum was phoning again, but the ship had sailed, no point, no sense in any further attempts to contact her son. Smell of petrol made her wretch as she sat in the comfortable arm-chair, as Simon continued to stare into the room, dead in the photograph.

Aiden wasn't looking at the ground as Dad came towards him, just looking straight at Dad in the dusk with the world around fading and the stones turning to shadows. Presently, Dad stopped walking. He was now standing about ten feet away.

'I've got something to show you; come with me.'

'Where?'

'Just come over here, do as your Dad tells you.'

'Mum will be worried. We need to get home... will you come home with me?'

'Not just yet, come over here, Aiden.'

Walking towards his Dad seemed very natural. After all, wasn't that what sons did when asked by their Dad? Within a minute, he was standing next to the figure that was his Dad, the smell of petrol now so strong yet so easy to ignore.

'Look, Aiden... look at the sky.'

Dad moved aside, and Aiden was at the top of H'ell Tor, and the sky opened up behind the highest rock on the hill.

And there was the rainbow riding in the space of twilight. Soaring above the barely visible patch of Skip Tor, above the black hulk of a Dartmoor shoulder, there was a rainbow... a proper rainbow. Nearest the horizon, it was the same shade as the sky, but then came all the colours, all the familiar colours in concentric shells, ever more luminous, and the last of them was a roaring red, a blood-like red that burned with a slice of fire. Rainbow of light, like a firework with all the rainbow colours, from out of nowhere, rainbow burning into the growing night, cannot be... surely cannot be a rainbow at the beginning of the night!

'A rainbow, but that's impossible! It's almost dark!' And there is no rain to make it!'

The bow of light displayed indistinct termini, like a real rainbow, the limbs descending into the gloom of Earth, to the right sinking to the low ground in the lee of the Common... to the left, merging into the Moor itself, light into darkness, The summit of glory rose directly above the shadows of Skip Tor, so full of light-life, so painful to view and yet impossible to look away.

Mum was phoning the police... dialling 999 with a handkerchief over her face, held in place with her left hand as her right hovered and shook over the keys. A combination of the toxic atmosphere in the room and her own rampant thoughts of dread manufacturing a nauseous cocktail. Mothers always knew when something was wrong with their kids. She had known it with Simon, and she knew it again, now... same churning stomach threatening to explode, same throbbing head, same sense of hopeless fury and the impossibility of meaningful action.

'Impossible Rainbow, that's right, Aiden... Rainbow in the dark without any rain... come along, we should have a closer look...'

'You can't get close to a rainbow... it's impossible!'

'But we have already decided that the rainbow is impossible, so what have we got to lose?'

The two figures, man and boy, side by side walked together towards the arc.

'Hold my hand.'

Aiden reached out a hand, a very cold hand. Dad held it tight. Dad's hand was very cold, seemed cold even compared to his own.

'There's someone else here, Aiden, someone else that you should meet.'

'Who's that?'

'Just you wait and see. He's waiting for us at the end of the Impossible Rainbow.'

Dad laughed, a really hearty laugh. Aiden had never heard him laugh like that before.

'The rainbow is miles away.'

'It's closer than you think, Aiden.'

Karen Beard was a ranger for the Dartmoor National Park authority, and she was out early on this morning. Unexceptionally so as Karen was very much an early morning kind of person. Early forties, fit as a fiddle, or so she liked to think, member of the gym at Sanderstone, ran marathons and then some, played badminton three times a week, at least. Currently living alone, and contentedly so. Good job that she was happy to be out early. An alert had come into her phone at seven a.m., reporting the sighting of a possible fire in the vicinity of H'ell Tor on the previous night. A local farmer had seen "some strange light on the hill" while checking sheep in the lee of Skip Tor, and had submitted a report to that effect to the Rangers. There had been a delay in circulating the details of the report. Strange that it had come to her, she was based on the other side of the Moor; this wasn't her patch, no matter, what was done was done.

Probably a bit late in the day if there had really been a fire, Karen had assessed. However, a report was a report and needed to be followed up... and so here she was on a freezing cold morning, atop H'ell Tor, wrapped in as many layers as she had been able to get her hands on.

Watch informed the time... eight-thirty... it had taken a while to get round, four-by-four had been a bugger to get going, everything had been iced-up from the night's sharp frost, even the garage accommodation afforded to the motor had not protected it from the freeze. No evidence of any fire; it was light enough at eight-thirty, even at this time of year, to spot any evidence of fire... no charring of the snowy ground.

Karen suddenly realised that there could never have been a fire... everywhere was coated with snow and ice... there couldn't have been a fire... the farmer must have been mistaken, though this was odd because farmers, more than most, were familiar with the comings and goings of the countryside, unlikely to make up phantom fires. Maybe HQ had misinterpreted the call, "strange light" did not a fire mean.

Close to the top of the hill, Karen noticed the tracks. They had come up the hill from the direction of Flashcombe.

Tracks made by the boots of a walker, looked quite small, probably a child's tracks, very distinct, outline frozen into place by the night-time frost, obviously formed recently. This was potentially a cause for concern... lone walker recently out in this weather and maybe still out... she should follow them, see where they led. Karen hoped against hope that the end of the trail would not be accompanied by the discovery of an injured boy or girl... or something even worse.

Tracks were joined by a second thread within ten yards.

These were very different.

These seemed to just start, as if whatever had made them had dropped out of the sky, parachuted down, into that place.

Each print was maybe four inches long and three inches wide, being some eighteen inches apart.

Deep-set into the snow, each bore the trace of two toes, something like a hoof.

Karen's face screwed up beneath the woolly hat. That couldn't be right, must have been a new-fangled walking boot that made those.

Thinking optimistically, at least the child, if it was a child... the maker of the first set of prints... had not been alone after all. Karen strode on through the deep snow on the crest of H'ell Tor, close to the topmost stone.

Then came a third set of tracks, these made by very small feet, by a young child, smaller, therefore younger than the first... again seemingly dropped in from God knows where. Karen Beard knew a thing or two about prints, animal, and human, having seen many of both types over the years, and the lines of human prints, made by booted feet, set into the snow, appeared familiar enough. As for the other set, the hoof-like marks, she hadn't seen anything quite like those... the sense that they were somehow "burned" into the snow, almost a branding, created a hint of unreality, an undefinable anxiety. The human prints, all ever so normal, showed the expected right-left progression whilst the 'other' tracks seemed to follow one-after-another, in single file... no hoofed animal known to Karen Beard left its marks in single file.

Three lines of walkers, two children on either side of something else, either side of some maker of angry, two-toed echoes, all walking together, past the topmost stone toward the lip of the summit, beyond which the moorland dropped away into the bowl sleeping below the Tor.

Karen continued to follow the tracks as they ran away on the falling ground... beyond this combe, the Moor rose again to the mighty summit of Skip Tor... that was half-a-mile away. Heart began to sink; this could be a big job... she felt duty-bound to follow these tracks, but where were they going, and when would they end? The presence of multiple humans made her more confident of a happy ending, so maybe she could bale out. Of course, she wouldn't. Beneath a deep blue sky with the sun so low it was barely a player in this extraordinary scene, she carefully negotiated the steep slope. Three sets of prints continued to draw her on, the odd hoof-print like impressions between the more conventional human-like tracks, and then suddenly they weren't there any more.

Ground was less steep at this point. At Karen's feet was a square patch of moorland moss, no snow here, patch must have been five feet square... and it was square, a perfect square. On this side, there were the prints; on the other, nothing, just snow, just a white blanket like everywhere else.

Why was there no snow on this patch... and what happened to the tracks? Couldn't just vanish. Karen stood and stared at the ground as if doing so would somehow change something. It didn't. She glanced around, looked up at the sky, looked at the sky above Skip Tor.

What should she do?

Never seen anything like this before, not in the five years she had been in the job. Sky above Skip Tor appeared strange, almost as if a rainbow was trying to form, but that was impossible... there was no rain.

Dark
Horse

It often takes the Impossible some time to arrive.
But when it does...

'So, you know the score then, chaps, do you not?'

The two men looked at each other, and then at the speaker, and then nodded.

The speaker smiled at them both... how ridiculous they looked... a couple of nodding donkeys, donkey being an appropriate description. He was very good at working people out, and he had worked these two out early doors. Adrian was an idiot, no doubt about it, miracle that he'd hung on this long. Blake was a different animal, not stupid, not stupid like Adrian, just lazy... no, that wasn't the right word, not lazy, maybe unfocussed was a better word, scatty, hair-brained, quite a talker but not worth listening to. Neither of them exactly officer material. Put them together and you might get something promising, but separately, no, not really. Both were one rung down the management ladder from the "Director of Administration" job that had become vacant following the departure of Bob Symes. Bob had received an offer that he couldn't refuse... more money and fewer hours. Adrian and

Blake currently ran other sections within the company, Adrian in HR, while Blake oversaw Communications. So it was that one of these modest talents was about to be shortly promoted, had to be one of them, no-one else at the front of the taxi-queue, no other Buggins available, it had to be one of these two.

'So, Frank, when will we know which of us is going to get the job?' Adrian asked. Adrian was a short, cylindrical kind of idiot, thirty-five, very pale, always seemed to sweat a lot, maybe he knew that he was an idiot. Suit always seemed two sizes too big for him. Even if he wore a suit two sizes smaller, it would look two sizes too big for him. Garishly coloured tie wasn't tied properly. The knot was too far down his shirt front, made him resemble a small-time impresario. Hair was curly and short, and the eyes small and rodentish. Frank Salmon peered over his glasses and didn't say anything at all for exactly ten seconds.

He then stood up and walked to the window. Big man was Frank, suit always seemed two sizes too small for him. Even if he had worn a suit two sizes bigger, it would have looked two sizes too small for him. Bald-headed, six-feet six in his socks, fifty last birthday (he and Martha had celebrated with a weekend in Barcelona, still displayed a legacy tan from the holiday before that (Barbados)). Very small ears, far too small for his head, teeth weren't too good, should get them fixed but there was never enough time. What with the work and the holidays, there was never enough time. Frank looked out of the window, seemingly fascinated by some event in the car park outside. Whatever it was took exactly twenty seconds to play out.

'Soon, Adrian, can't say exactly, but certainly... soon.'

'Before the end of the year?'

Frank considered his response for five seconds.

'What date is it now?'

'It's the tenth of October.'

'Tenth of October... yes, I should think that the board will have decided by the end of the year... great Christmas present for somebody, eh chaps?'

Adrian smiled.

Blake didn't.

Frank looked at Blake. Blake wasn't behaving in the way that he, Frank, might have expected. As far as the promotion was concerned, there was only one winner as far as Frank was concerned, but it wasn't his decision entirely. Frank had expected Blake to do a lot of talking at this meeting because that was what Blake usually did, nonsense most of it, not worth listening to, most of it, but it was reassuring nonsense because it was expected. A silent Blake was unexpected, and therefore, for Frank, disturbing.

'You aren't saying much, Blake, everything all right?'

Blake nodded.

'Fine Frank... thanks for being so er... frank.'

'Nice one, Blake,' Adrian turned and smiled a death-smile at his new adversary.

'Very droll, Blake... now, does anyone have any other questions?'

'Anyone' wasn't the right word, there were only two of them, but Frank was unsettled by Blake not acting like Blake and couldn't find the correct expression.

'Good Show, if no-one has any other questions then...?'

He looked at Blake, wiling him to say something else, 'Bloody say something, Blake,' he didn't say. Blake then said something.

'What will we be judged on, Frank? Are there any particular qualities that the board will be looking for?'

This was more like it.

'Usual stuff, Blake... decision-making, leadership, grasp of strategy, team player, that kind of bullshit, I should add that there will be no interviews...we already know you both very well.'

'Sounds like a fight to the death,' Blake replied. He should then probably have smiled in order to confirm the levity of the statement but did not, thus creating a slight chill in the air.

'Oh, I wouldn't say that... no-one dies through not getting promoted,' Frank beamed, though due to his poor teeth, the effect was not as intended. The mass of flesh that was Frank then relocated to his executive chair, behind his executive desk. There was a "wumph" kind of noise as he sank into the leather. Placing his hands, fingers spread widely, on top of his desk, he stared at his subordinates, head rocking from side to side.

'Good Show, right, if no-one has any other questions then...?'

Silence, and then the man in charge had an idea. It made him smile again.

'As I said, no-one dies through not getting promoted, not even at "Simkins".' That smile again. 'You should both shake hands... may the best man win, but whoever that may be, both of you will continue to make "Simkins" proud, I'm confident of that.'

Adrian and Blake looked at each other, at that moment not entirely sure whether the proposition was serious, expressions reflecting their confusion. Frank's head continued to oscillate from left to right, waiting for some action, but action did not come.

'Come on, chaps, shake hands!'

The protagonists awkwardly twisted towards each other in their chairs, hands meeting over the void. A limp connection followed, a meeting of the hands if not the minds.

'Well done, well done, well... off you go then, go back to your offices and prepare for promotion... or not, as the case may be.'

'The bastard is enjoying this... the bastard is really enjoying this, the bastard,' thought Blake as they both left.

'After you,' Adrian beckoned Blake through the exit... thus demonstrating both assertiveness and team-playing... that's two boxes ticked then.

The journey back to their respective offices proved a silent voyage, Adrian and Blake staring straight ahead, both grateful for the opportunity to say 'hi' to that moron, Dennison, as he passed them by. Dennison was the new boy... won't be the new boy for long, thought Blake, not if Frank has any sense, or maybe it would be up to him to let the idiot go... if he got the promotion. Saying 'hi' to Dennison broke the ice wall that both connected and separated Blake and Adrian as they walked along the corridor, Adrian and Blake heading West, that fool Dennison heading East. Adrian's 'hi' was accompanied by a smile, easy to smile at an idiot if you are an idiot yourself, thought Blake, there being no smile attached to his own greeting. For himself, a nod would suffice, had to make sure that the new boy knew his place, planning for the future, just in case...

Not a long walk, this one, for Adrian and Blake, and wouldn't you know it, they were next-door neighbours, no, no man's land separating these close combatants, merely a wall, and a thin one at that, for they occupied adjacent offices.

The company was a local institution here in the town of Farely, Farely in Stedfordshire, the heart of the English Midlands with the county town (Stedford) a mere ten miles away. Maybe very large village would be a better label for Farely as it did not host many of the amenities normally associated with a proper town. There wasn't a "Costa" or a "Starbucks" in the place, and certainly not a "Café Nero". In Stedford, by contrast, there were all of these. In fact, there were two "Costas", one near the marketplace and one in the just-out-of-town retail park. There was a "Wetherspoons" in Stedford as well. For Adrian, that was a positive; he liked "Wetherspoons"... this one was called "The Silver Arrow", strange name for a pub, but it was nice in there, often took the wife in on a Saturday. There wasn't a "Wetherspoons" in Farely, and there wasn't much prospect of one any time soon.

Blake didn't much like "Wetherspoons"; he was more of an "old-fashioned local" kind of drinker. The absence of a "Wetherspoons" in Farely didn't bother Blake in the slightest... he had his local, and that was good enough for him.

As Blake entered his tiny office, he noted the time. He possessed a non-company issue wall-clock, just to the left of his desk, and it was sending a message... five-thirty, time to go home, time to pick up the coat and bag. If he was quick, he could slip out before Adrian (who would also be leaving at this time), and then he wouldn't have to say goodbye. Fatally, in his hurry, he dropped his bag on the way out... tried to turn out the light with the same hand as was holding the bag, big mistake. Those precious, lost seconds meant that he and Adrian departed their offices at exactly the same time, so he should probably say goodbye to Adrian after all.

He would do so, but only after they had both left the building.

Two human souls, so connected and yet so apart, strode, side-by-side, silently, along the barren, white, over-illuminated corridor. The offices of Adrian and Blake were located on the second floor of the grim edifice that housed "Simkins", the journey to the exit taking them to the lift at the very end of the passage... a route passing Frank Salmon's office. A terrible thought swam into Blake's brain. What if Frank came out? What if Frank had decided to go home at the same time as Adrian and himself? The three of them would be walking to the end of the corridor, heading for the lift... that would be proper grim, three non-amigos exuding mutual hostility.

He could take the stairs, the stairwell was next to the lift, but that would appear an obvious slight... and anyway, chances were that Adrian and Frank would emerge from the lift just as he, Blake, alighted on the ground floor, that would be just too awkward. As it turned out, Frank didn't appear, though it was a close-run thing, Blake could hear the scraping of a chair from within the office as he and his new nemesis hurried by... the Salmon was preparing to leave the building. Increasing his pace yet further in a desperate effort to avoid a meeting, he began to leave Adrian behind also. Adrian wasn't walking as quickly as he, Blake... maybe Adrian wasn't as fearful of a meeting with Salmon... maybe he even *wanted* a meeting? Just by "accident"? 'Oh, Hello, Frank, nice to see you... about this promotion...,' that kind of meeting.

He slowed down, ensuring that they both reached the lift at the same time. In the lift, in the cage, it was very bad. Blake even considered saying something but couldn't think of anything to say. Shouldn't be for him to start the conversation in any case. He noted that Adrian appeared to be sweating... nerves, thought Blake. Turned out that Adrian was more unsettled than he was by this short-term close encounter. He, Blake, wasn't showing it, no perspiration on this boy. Lift opened on the ground floor. Five seconds to get across the lobby and then out of the revolving doors... designed to keep the heat in though folk always abused the situation by using the automatic swing door nearby, the one that was meant to be used by disabled visitors. Blake didn't. Blake always used the revolving doors.

'See you tomorrow.'

'Yes, see you tomorrow, have a good evening,' Adrian replied.

The concrete horror that housed "Simkins" stood at the junction of Jamieson Street, Mill Street, and Stable Road. On leaving the building (preposterously named "Simkins House" on a small notice set into the plot's boundary wall), Blake headed to the right and Adrian to the left.

Adrian lived on the western edge of the village, on River Lane, named for a rather pathetic stream that followed the line of the road. Blake had visited on one occasion, long time ago, shortly after Adrian had joined "Simkins". When had that been, maybe eight or ten years ago? Something like that. Adrian had invited himself and the Mrs over to celebrate a birthday... just the kind of thing one does in a new job, try to convince everyone that you're one of the lads, just the once... then the desire dissolves. There's only so much glad-handing of work 'colleagues' that a grown man can take, just the one party and let that be the end of it.

Blake speeded up to increase the distance between himself and Adrian as quickly as possible. If two people are walking quickly in opposite directions, it doesn't take long for them to be satisfyingly apart. Turning sharp left into Brook Lane, he was now most definitely out of sight of Adrian. There would be no more Adrian until tomorrow, and even then, maybe no Adrian. There was no inevitability of seeing Adrian tomorrow, despite them being next-door neighbours.

Slowing up, the strides became steps, then it started to rain, and he realised that he had left the brolly in the office... a negative consequence of his over-hasty departure. Never mind, it wasn't raining very much. Blake looked skywards, it was still BST, but the shower had made the overhead darker than it should be. Back towards the West, towards Adrian country, there was a purple band of nearly-light, a promise of very late sunshine, but above looked full of rain, frequency of the drops... and their size, increasing. Blake once more accelerated, not too far to walk or run... now at the end of

Brook Lane with all the posh houses and left again into his road, his road being Milton Close.

Milton Close was a very short Close, and he lived at its very end, in the very last house, should get a real hurry-on now, but then again, if you are already wet, what is the point? You can only be so wet. If you are wet, you are wet. Such were the pointless thoughts that wandered across the brain of Blake Roberts as he opened the gate ... soon be inside. All the downstairs lights were on, Lorna was at home, good, she had made it before him, and so he would benefit from getting home when all the downstairs lights were already on, and there would be someone to welcome him across the threshold.

Adrian looked around at the very moment that Blake turned sharp left into Brook Lane, couldn't help breathing a sigh of relief, stupid really... Blake couldn't do anything to hurt him. Blake could not do him harm unless being promoted instead of him was doing harm. Should have brought an umbrella. It had started raining... looked like it could be a proper shower, blast, too late now.

Straight down Jamieson Street it was for Adrian Golgarry. Just keep on walking until the houses ran out, and then, on the right and across the road, a concealed entrance... River Lane, struggling to make itself seen within a copse of oaks, seemingly all growing far too close together to be healthy, and what little space there was between the twisted trunks filled with subordinate bushes reaching upwards, desperate for a taste of clean air and sunlight. Adrian had to cross the road in order to access the entrance to River Lane, and he always, purely through habit, left this action until the last possible moment. Just as he turned to cross, a car loomed in the corner of his vision. Pausing on the edge of the kerb, he waited for it to pass... as it did so, the driver hooted. Adrian waved as the vehicle haired off down the road... didn't recognise the car or the driver; maybe it was some idiot trying to upset him. Shouldn't have waved, shouldn't have responded at all, too late now.

A rough footpath on the right-hand side of River Lane would take him home. It was raining hard now, though the trees were providing some cover. A minute or two's stiff walking later, the road and associated footpath burst out of the shelter into more open country, a row of detached houses ahead of him, his own being the second one along. Without the canopy above, he was fair game for the downpour, but it didn't much matter now because he was pretty much back at barracks. The lights were on in the house... looks like Claire had made it home first... good, always nice to walk into a house with all the lights on, thought Adrian.

Turning right into the footpath, he headed for the front door... should probably take the garden furniture into the garage... job for the weekend, certainly not for now. Quite fancied a gin and tonic right now. Key was in his pocket somewhere, might be quicker to ring the doorbell, but then again Claire might be in the kitchen making dinner, here's hoping. Hard to hear the doorbell in the kitchen, should probably have a look at that, thought Adrian, maybe another job for the weekend. Found the key eventually, and then inside.

'Hi, Claire, I'm home.'

On the other side of the door was a tiny entrance hall, to the right was the front room and to the left there was the kitchen. Directly ahead was the staircase to the upstairs. All the lights were indeed on, but there was currently silence in Golgarry Towers.

'Claire, where are you?'

Then a faint rumbling noise, the sound of a distant train on distant tracks, a rumbling noise from upstairs.

'Are you upstairs?'

Adrian stalked to the bottom of the stairs, shaking off excess water as he went, rather in the manner of a hairy dog. He stood and looked up, 'Claire!'

Then she appeared at the end of the short stretch of wooden railing on the landing.

'Hello, Adrian.'

'What are you up to... sounds like you've got someone else up there, what's he doing... heading for the drain-pipe?'

Claire smiled, recognising a familiar strain in her husband's humour, 'He's just left.'

'Hope he's got a brolly. It's pouring down.'

'So, I see,' Claire swept down the stairs into the light. Short, very blond hair cut similarly, amazingly expressive eyes of some indeterminate colour, not brown or green but somehow all of these, and more. She still wore most of her work clothes... Claire was employed as a receptionist at the surgery in Stedford. Work clothes were dark skirt and dark jacket, though she had taken the jacket off.

'So?'

'So what?'

She was now standing beside him.

'So, how did the meeting go?'

'Oh... that!'

'Yes, that.'

'Let's go into the front room.'

He always called it the front room, never the lounge, must have been a result of his humble upbringing... Dad would never have used the term "lounge".

'I fancy a G&T.'

'Really... but we've not had dinner yet.'

'I've had a trying day, Claire... the least that a working man can expect at the end of a trying day is a kiss from the wife and a G&T.'

'Yes, but what about you?'

Adrian smiled, recognising a familiar strain in his wife's humour.

'Very droll.'

The front room/lounge was an unexpectedly large space, if one's expectations were solely based on the dimensions of the entrance hall. A large bay window looked out onto the front garden, with the sight of furniture again reminding Adrian of work yet to do. Various items of house-furniture were distributed around the room, sofa (not couch), cabinets, armchairs (two), standard lamp which was never turned on, table with a fruit bowl that had never hosted any fruit... and two ash-trays, though neither Claire nor Adrian had ever smoked. Television on another table, almost underneath the window but the top of which was just about visible from the outside. The TV faced inwards, not like those houses where random pedestrians could watch the thing from the pavement because the TV screen was fully visible from outside.

Claire opened one of the cabinet's front doors. They called it a drinks cabinet... inside, there were bottles... gin, vodka, tonic, whisky... just for the benefit of visitors.

'G&T eh, are you sure?'

'Why don't you have one?'

'I'm not sure... I've got work tomorrow.'

'For God's sake, woman, one gin-and-tonic is not going to wipe you out tomorrow morning is it?... do you want one or not? If you don't, fine, but don't not have one because of tomorrow morning... I mean!'

Claire turned the right-most corner of her mouth up, a signal of consternation that was familiar to her husband. In sympathy, Adrian's own lips twisted into a slope, running down from left to right, a signal of regret that was familiar to his wife.

'Sorry... it's been a long day.'

'So how did it go then?' The words uttered as the drink was poured, all climaxed by a fizzing noise as the bottle of tonic was expertly opened, Claire was great at gin-and-tonics.

'Shame we don't have an ice machine,' Adrian declared before descending into his favourite armchair... both armchairs were identical, but he still had a favourite, the one nearest the television. Hard to see the television from this armchair, but no matter, there was rarely anything worth watching.

'OK, I think... seems that Frank... or somebody... ' at this, Adrian's voice tailed off, and his eyes strayed to the window. Then he took a sip from the glass, 'Very nice.'

'So, what happened?... actually, I will have one, bugger it!' Claire, still standing at this stage, took two steps to the cabinet and began to create her own G&T.

'Looks like it's a fight between me and Blake for the job... one of us shall become the "Director of Administration"!' The last part of this sentence being amplified as the first alcohol molecules arrived at the appropriate receptors in the mind of the male Golgarry.

'What do you mean?'

'One of us will get it... may the best man win!'

'Sounds a bit weird.'

'Frank Salmon is weird.'

'Did you talk about it with Blake?'

Adrian looked down into his lap, wherein lay his precious G&T.

'Not really. After all, we are now adversaries... are we not?'

'But you get on well with Blake, don't you?'

'Maybe, maybe not.' Adrian was more taken with the 'maybe not' but didn't fancy a discussion on the issue.

'So... do you think you're in with a chance?'

'Doubt it... Frank thinks I'm an idiot... it's obvious. Thinks that the sun shines out of Blake's... well, he thinks a lot of Blake.'

'You're no idiot.'

'Thanks,' Adrian took another very large sip.

'You're not drinking your wallop.' He noted disapprovingly.

'I'm listening to you, Adrian, this is important... this is a promotion. Surely you realise that this is important.'

'Yes.'

There followed a moment of silence as multiple sips were taken by both parties.

'You should try and break down the barriers between you and Frank.'

'How do you mean?'

'Convince Frank that you're one of the boys... a team player.'

These words slightly confused Adrian, weren't the kind of words that Claire normally used.

Fact was that Claire quite liked the prospect of her husband to be possessed with the label "Director of Administration"... who wouldn't? The extra salary would come in handy for her grand plan.

'Not sure that would work.'

'Don't know until you try.'

'What's for dinner, anyway?' Adrian had emptied his G&T and fancied a second... doubting that this idea would fly before dinner. He determined that the meal should be executed with all speed so he could have another drink.

'No idea... it's your turn to make it.'

Adrian had forgotten about this, inwardly cursing he rapidly played for time.

'And how did your day go?'

'Hello, Lorna, I'm home!'

Blake crossed the threshold gratefully as the rain continued to teem down.

Lorna came out of the lounge and gave him a hug.

'How was your day?' He enquired. Lorna taught at Stedford primary.

'Fine, except that the car was misbehaving earlier.'

'What was the problem?'

'Rattling noise in the engine.'

Lorna was short, blessed with the most gorgeous ginger hair, that had clinched it for Blake all those years ago.

'Rattling noise in the engine... what's that s'posed to mean?'

'Means what it says... fancy a drink before dinner?'

'I'm OK, thanks... maybe later.'

'I think I'll have one... Simon had a fit this afternoon, caused mayhem in the class, kids in tears.'

'Sounds like you deserve one.'

By this time, the two Roberts were standing in the lounge, Lorna making for the drinks' cabinet as Blake sank into the three-seater sofa... overkill as there was only two of them, couldn't remember why they had opted for a three-seater. The sound of the whisky and soda being prepared made him feel happy... looked forward to making his own later.

'What's for dinner?'

'I beg your pardon?'

'What's...,' then he was struck by the awful thought... it was his turn to make dinner. He had intended to leave work early, but what with the meeting with Frank... 'Bugger, it's my turn, isn't it?'

'Yes.'

'Do you know what? I really fancy some fish and chips.'

'Do you really?' Lorna was sitting next to him, very close; bodies were touching in all sorts of places. 'Odd, every time it's your turn to make dinner, you fancy fish and chips.'

'What a coincidence... anyway. What do you think?'

'S'pose so.'

'I'll go and get 'em.'

'Bloody right you will.'

Blake stood up, full of intent.

'Before you go... how did the meeting with Frank go... what was it all about?'

Blake crossed mental fingers... he had known what the meeting was going to be about in advance but had decided to keep that to himself. In retrospect, he could just have not mentioned it at all but had given the game away at the weekend.

'Got a meeting with Frank on Wednesday,' he'd said, after a few beers in the "Dark Horse"... that had been on Saturday night.

'What about?' Lorna had enquired. Blake had made an executive decision to lie at that point. Didn't want an excellent evening spoiled by talk of promotion... should never have mentioned it in the first place.

'Not sure.'

The conversation had then moved on. Now there was no hiding place.

'It was about a forthcoming promotion,' Lorna picked up the vibe immediately. Blake often used long and improbable words when he was nervous, 'forthcoming' not a part of his normal vocabulary. Nevertheless, she was intrigued by that word 'promotion'.

'Promotion... eh?'

Blake returned to his seat.

'Yep.'

He realised that he needed to tell the story in full, and so proceeded to do so.

'You and Adrian... that's a no-brainer!'

'I'm not so sure... I might have a chance.'

'Silly bugger... you know what I mean.'

Blake smiled and stood up again, 'I should probably try

and make sure I get it, I mean, as you say, in terms of ability and sheer quality, I would get the job no problem,' he was being facetious, and the message was duly received, 'Sometimes though, the best man doesn't always win.'

He left the thought hanging in the air as he headed for the door.

'Where are you going?'

'Upstairs.'

'Why?'

'This is my... our house. I can go upstairs if I want, can't I?'

'But we haven't finished the conversation.'

'I'm going to fetch my other brolly, left one at work... you still want chips, don't you?'

Blake was already halfway up the stairs as the last words of chastisement drifted across the room, and so he felt no need to respond. Once upstairs, he headed for the marital bedroom, there being a second available for the use of guests, not that they had any very often. Inside, he picked up the deputy umbrella. It was lying against the tall mirror next to the dressing table... and there he was in the mirror, in all his glory.

Just kind of average, average height, five-six, not too thick and not too thin, brown hair, looked quite smart at the moment, just had it cut... could look fly-away and wispy if left untrimmed, nose was a little sharper than was normal, but that was hardly his fault... didn't wear spectacles but probably should do, putting off the inevitable but never mind. Stooped a little, maybe that made him look older than his years, his forty years, he knew that he was older than Adrian, not too much older? Was that a plus or a minus in regard to the current theatre, maybe both, maybe neither, maybe he should just pick up the brolly and go and get the chips. Farewell to the guy in the mirror, then, and back downstairs. The telly was on, could hear its low murmur as he descended. Glanced at his watch, it was six-thirty, what would be on... the local news on BBC1, Lorna always watched BBC1, no imagination. Sure enough, back in the lounge, there she was, perched on the sofa like a kingfisher about to pick up a salmon... salmon... couldn't get him out of his head, there he was, large as life, Frank Salmon, gills flexing as the mouth opened and closed, searching for the next second of life...

'There you are. I thought you'd fallen asleep.'

Again, Blake did not bite, the query sounding to him, rhetorical.

'Just chips?'

She glanced away from the screen, 'What?'

'Do you want chips, or fish and chips, or what do you want?'

'Fish and chips.'

'Well, well, you've changed your tune, haven't you... hammering me a minute ago, and now you're all for it.'

'Actually, I was just thinking.'

Blake was preparing to leave... glancing out of the window he saw that it wasn't raining. Typical, maybe he should leave the brolly at home... but it could start again; he would take it just in case. 'What thoughts have you had?'

'I was just thinking... about your promotion... you might invite Adrian along to the "Dark Horse"... that might set the ball rolling, might give him something to think about.'

Blake paused, suspending his window-watching.

'That's quite a good thought...' Indeed the thought caused him to become somewhat animated, '... As a matter of fact, there may well be an opportunity coming up. Next Tuesday, we're both signed up to a course at the Business Hub that's just round the corner from the "Horse"... I could suggest we go there after it finishes, on the way home, so to speak.'

'Sounds like it was meant to be.'

'Wouldn't go that far.'

Lorna merely turned and looked back at the screen, Blake following her eyes to see the image of a cat with a heavily bandaged front leg. Time to leave. Temporarily parking the brolly against the doorframe, he exited the lounge, pausing only to grab a jacket before stepping into the outdoors, almost forgetting the brolly.

Not too far to the chip shop and Blake was pleased to see that, though the sky was darkening, the clouds from earlier had broken up, the prospect of any further rain consequently diminished. Back he walked, back along Milton Close, right into Brook Lane for about fifty metres then across the road into Fisher Close wherein lay a small number of retail units, a hairdressers (unisex but Blake always went to a place he liked in Stedford when he needed his done), a bookies (never had a bet and wouldn't know how to), a newsagent run by Mr Kalinsky, a place that sold washing machines whose survival as a viable concern was itself a miracle... and a chippy. Small, functional, very white, and with one of those blue arcs that were supposed to kill insects painlessly. Pull the poor buggers in with the lure of light, and then "zap", frying tonight, sure enough governor. On this night, inside the "Never Haddock So Good" fish and chip emporium, there was a queue of one, an old gentleman who appeared vaguely familiar to Blake, maybe he had seen him in here before, looked like he was already being attended to. The old-timer turned round to face the new arrival, confronting Blake with a very lived-in face, wrinkles within wrinkles, looking out from beneath an equally lived-in black, flat cap.

'Some weather... eh?' The old gentleman nodded towards the window.

Blake smiled.

'Raining cats and dogs earlier... eh?'

Blake smiled again.

'Salt and vinegar?' Both customers jumped very slightly, Mr Haddock's voice often causing folk to startle, it being very deep and loud and sonorous, befitting of a man of significant girth. Mr Haddock was certainly well-endowed with girth, and height, and most other dimensions. Face was so red it was close to purple, and very pitted, looked as battered as one of his cod fillets. Mr Haddock was not his real name of course, Blake didn't know his real name, but did think of him as an acquaintance, being a regular customer and all that.

'Yes, please', said the old gentleman.

The large man in white overalls liberally splashed salt and vinegar over the generous portion of cod and chips.

'That all?'

'Yes, thank you.'

The difference between the croaky tones of the old gentleman and the bass of Mr Haddock appeared to demonstrate the full spectrum of the human voice in just two humans.

'Call it a fiver.'

No credit or debit cards at "Haddock's", a sign on the counter told the story... or at least a part of it, the "C" had fallen away and so the instruction declared, "ash Only". The old gentleman dug around in the right-hand pocket of his cardigan, the cardigan was beneath his coat, and so the operation was complex, taking several minutes to execute. Old Gentleman knew he had a fiver there somewhere... it was always a fiver at Mr Haddock's, and so that was what he always brought... ah, got it! Fiver duly handed over from a claw-like hand.

'And what can I get you?'

That question was directed at Blake.

'Cod and chips, twice.'

'I heard you the first time.'

Old Gentlemen, almost out of the door at this stage,

148

paused and laughed uproariously, a lot more volume than Blake had expected, couldn't help smiling himself. Mr Haddock also chuckled, despite himself, as he gathered the items together.

'Sorry,' said Old Gentleman, now on his way out, making room for an incoming customer.

'Well, well, hello Blake!'

'Hello, Adrian.'

''Bye all,' said Old Gentleman.

'Fancy us both coming out for fish and chips... small world, eh?'

'Indeed.' Adrian was wearing an inappropriately long grey coat, the kind that bookmakers are often believed to wear, and carried a furled-up umbrella. The latter looked like it might have writing on it, but this was indecipherable in its current, folded state.

'Salt and vinegar?'

'Yes, on both.'

'Right you are.'

'Just fancied some fish and chips, mentioned it to Claire, and she felt the same way.'

'Well, well,' hard to conceal the boredom and the annoyance. What was he doing here? He lived miles away... He must have a more local chippy than this one?

'Didn't think you were a fish and chip kind of person, to be honest, Blake, thought you might be...'

'... Call it a tenner.' Mr Haddock brutally interrupted, Blake handing over a crisp note.

'Keep the change,' he said. Mr Haddock chuckled as he deposited the cash in an old-fashioned till that made a "ching" noise as the drawer snapped shut. He then turned his attention to the new customer... 'And yourself?'

'Same again.'

'Right you are,' Mr Haddock's script appeared to be rather limited.

'Blake, I was wondering.'

'What about?'

'Just that, I was just thinking that we might go out for a beer some time.'

This "wondering" had been precipitated by Claire's suggestion of the "team-player" project. Maybe a few ales in Blakes' throat would lubricate the lips and initiate the spilling of some unsavoury beans. Maybe Blake would give something away, say something unwise, maybe he would be indiscreet. This malevolent seed had germinated within Adrian's head on the way to the chippy.

Blake couldn't believe his luck.

'I think that sounds like a great plan... must be ages since we went for beers.'

Adrian smiled. This was going very well.

'Salt and vinegar?'

'Yes, please, on both.'

'Right you are.'

Blake needed to get away. Chips would get cold if he was unduly delayed.

'We have this thing on at the Business Hub next Tuesday. We could go out after that.'

Adrian felt a warm glow flooding through his being, 'Yes, great idea.'

'Call it a tenner.' Haddock handed over the parcel of food.

'Sorry.' Now it was his turn to hand over the note. Mr Haddock eyed this with suspicion.

'Hang on... this is a Scottish tenner... you trying to swindle me?'

Adrian's face turned almost as purple as Mr Haddock's.

'You can accept them... they are legal tender.' He cursed inwardly. Where had that come from... someone must have passed it to him.

'You can only use that if you're buying haggis,' roared Mr

Haddock, 'and we don't sell that!'

Nevertheless, the Scottish tenner was imported to the till before Haddock retreated rapidly to a back room, no other customers having arrived.

'We could go to the "House of Cards", that's close to the Hub.'

'I know a place that's even closer,' Blake went for it.

'Where's that?'

'The "Dark Horse".'

'The "Dark Horse"?'

'That's what I said.'

'I've never heard of the "Dark Horse"... this was indeed true. Adrian, having lived at various locations in and about Farely, had never come across the "Dark Horse".

'It's on Stable Road, just round the corner from the Hub.'

Adrian squinted in concentration, 'I've walked down Stable Road a hundred times, there's no pubs down that way. You must be getting confused with some other place.'

'Gotta go, chips will be getting cold.'

Blake departed the "Never Haddock So Good" fish emporium and headed for home. Good job he had brought the umbrella... there were a few spots of rain in the air.

Time passed as it always does, the week swallowed up in the furnaces of time, and then it was the weekend, even by the standards of the Roberts' normal weekend, this one was unspectacular. On the Saturday afternoon, a new fridge was delivered, Lorna having decided that the old one simply wasn't big enough.

'How come it's not big enough?' Blake had protested, when the proposal had first emerged, several weeks earlier. But Lorna had her way, as she usually did. On the Sunday afternoon, the two of them had gone for a walk, ending up at the Station Fields on the edge of the village, close to where the old railway station once stood. These days it was parkland, with a small caravan site in one corner that the Gypsies sometimes used.

'So, what did you think, did you find it useful?'

'Did *you*?'

Blake replied to Adrian's question with a question. They were standing in the tiny reception area of the Business Hub; almost everyone else had already gone home... "everyone else" being a small number. It was four-thirty on a Tuesday afternoon, a clock on the wall confirming the news.

The Hub reception was a square space with three doors leading off, one to a seminar room wherein the day's business had been hosted. Plastic imitation plants in plastic pots were liberally distributed around the garishly lit lobby... there was only one window (illumination came from startlingly bright spotlights, there being little natural light) and only three people left. The occasion had been the "Farely Business Outreach" event, "An Opportunity for Businesses based in Farely, and the Surrounding Area to Get Together and Discuss Issues that REALLY AFFECT THEM". The cold facts were that there weren't too many businesses in Farely, and so turnout had been modest.

The Business Hub was situated within a collection of old warehouses in a car park next to the Methodist Church, Blake suspecting that the incumbent congregation in the adjacent building was greater than that attending the "Farely Business Outreach" event. Two actual businesses operated out of the Hub, "Simmond's Signs" and a company that made fishing rods, whose name Blake could not recall.

He looked around. The only soul left apart from themselves was a short, curly-haired woman dressed in a black business suit, standing alone by the door and sipping from a bottle of water. She had been quite chatty in the post-lunch session, "Public Transport... How does it Affect WHAT YOU DO?" Complaining that it was difficult to get to her job at the Estate Agents where she worked because she didn't have a car, and the number seven bus was sometimes late, and sometimes it didn't turn up at all. She had been ticked off by Mr Marshall for being late, and once, she had to phone in and say she would have to take the day off because she simply couldn't get in.

What was her name again? She had been introduced, or rather she had introduced herself...

What was her name again?

Blake couldn't remember.

Maybe he should go across, maybe both he and Adrian should go across and break bread... but he really couldn't be bothered.

'Have you finished your coffee?'

Adrian had finished his coffee ages ago, had a talent for drinking hot coffee very quickly.

'Yep.'

'Fancy a pint in the "Dark Horse"? I've checked the weather forecast, and we should be OK.'

Adrian hadn't forgotten, he was expecting this invitation, hoping for this invitation, though he pondered on his companion's mention of the forecast for a moment... seemed a bit extreme, bearing in mind the pub would only be two minutes' walk away... if it existed at all... Adrian remaining unconvinced.

'Let's go.'

Blake nodded discretely at the curly-haired woman. Adrian didn't, just kept his eyes on the door. Curly-haired woman nodded back. The two men walked determinedly toward the exit.

'Bye-bye!'

Blake made his farewell rather loudly in the otherwise silent reception. The curly-haired woman smiled silently; maybe she had nothing left to say. Adrian finally tilted his head in her direction but also said nothing.

'We'll be into our first pints in three minutes,' said Blake, as the two swept out of the building... if you could call it a building. Once outside, they both let out a sigh. It was cool but bright. Wind was sweeping in from the South.

'I knew I should have bought a coat,' murmured Adrian melodramatically, wrapping his arms around his own body. They were both dressed in their office-best, dark suits and ties, looked like a couple of gangsters. Just needed the hats.

'No worries, it's just a couple of minutes' walk.'

Having exited the car park, it was sharp left on the street and then, almost before you knew it, sharp left again... into Stable Road.

'I've been down here loads of times...,' said Adrian, head rotating wildly... much more of this, and it would be a scene from the "Omen", '... And I've never seen a pub down here... this is ridiculous, Blake; there aren't any pubs down here... is this a wind-up?'

'Not at all.'

They walked on silently. A cyclist haired past them on the pavement, some expletive lost to the wind as if it was their fault.

'Drives me crazy, cyclists on the pavement.' Blake remarked, looking menacingly at the fast-disappearing man-cycle unit. Adrian wasn't listening.

'Where is this pub then?'

'Here it is.'

Blake abruptly stopped walking.

On the left, standing between two old, high, Victorian detached houses, was a curious box of a place. A square box, a two-storey box under a roof that was a perfect cone, one chimney poking out, to the right, just below the apex.

Smoke was coming out of the chimney!

Set back from the pavement, walls built of red brick with red tiles to make a roof, glowing in the light of the late day, two windows up and two down, like a house on the front of a biscuit tin.

There were curtains at the upstairs windows, red curtains, of course.

A path led to the door; there were strips of lawn on either side. Very well kept, nice lawns, well looked after by someone. In Adrian's mind, a domestic thought materialised pointlessly.

'We should make the garden look nice,' Claire had said on numerous occasions. Adrian couldn't make the garden look nice because he didn't know very much about gardens. Blake looked at Adrian. Adrian's face was a picture, though not the type you would see on the front of a biscuit tin.

'Are you OK? You look a bit pale?'

'Fine, fine, it's just...'

'Just what?'

Answer came there none.

Adrian was very discomforted, very upset, and very disorientated. There had never been a pub here, never, or any building at all. Between the two old, high, Victorian detached houses, there had always been a gap. He remembered it well. A gap with weeds poking out of cracked concrete, may have been a car park at one time but no more, now wasteland, a place for kids and the street-people, a place of beer-cans and blight.

He had been past here a hundred times, and there had never been a pub here.

But he was about to walk into it.

'My round,' said Blake as they walked towards the entrance.

The entrance was a door equidistant from the two ground

floor windows, centrally placed, so to speak.

To Blake's eyes, Adrian still appeared very pale, to be expected, of course, but he continued to say the right things.

'You sure you're OK?'

'Yes, yes.'

Blake, of course, was merely being mischievous. He had seen this reaction many times before, unsurprising, a perfectly natural reaction to a pub that was only there some of the time. An invitation to a pub that is only there some of the time is bound to elicit a reaction if the invitee is familiar with the neighbourhood. Adrian raised his eyes as they approached the threshold. The sign above the oak door, the kind of door that you might find in a castle, was very small, very small for a pub sign. He could just about read the golden letters embedded in the black plate.

"THE DARK HORSE".

'After you,' said Blake.

'We look a bit overdressed, don't you think?'

'Not at all... everyone's welcome in the "Dark Horse", even businessmen.'

Adrian pushed the door.

'Have to do better than that... give it a proper shove.'

He pushed again, it opened, and a blast of cold air hit him full in the face.

'Jesus, what was that?'

Inside, initially, all was dark, literally, black, nothing to be seen, but over a period of maybe half-a-minute, definition and light came and the place took on the appearance of a pub, with a bar to the right, and customers... but all of this took time to manifest itself. Sound rose in volume as the speakers kicked in.

The "Dark Horse" needed time to boot up.

'What can I get you?' Blake asked as they moved towards the bar.

Adrian looked around the place... still in a state of the state just below shock.

The bar area was square, the entrance through which they had come delivering them to the centre of the space. Chairs and tables were scattered around but not very many, Adrian counting about ten, many of which were occupied. There was the usual pub-mumble, nothing out of the ordinary, this was no "Slaughtered Lamb", no sudden silence or staring at the incomers. That was something to be welcomed, at least, thought Adrian. The bar counter to the right was devoid of custom, bar stools unoccupied. It was also devoid of a bartender. Blake appeared undeterred, continuing his enquiry.

'So, what do you want?'

Adrian's eyes were still exploring. A dartboard, directly opposite the entrance, was just visible in the inside-gloom. Blackboards on either side told the scores of old matches, but there were no darts being played tonight. What looked to Adrian very like an upright piano stood dangerously close to the dartboard... right in the zone for bounce-outs. Didn't see pianos in pubs very much these days.

'Anyone ever play the old Joanna?' He asked of his companion.

'Never seen anyone... hang on, the landlord's daughter had a go, once, lovely thing she was.'

The floor was tiled, the ceiling looked to be made of wood, but there were none of the false beams that decorated many faux-rustic drinking houses. This was a basic boozer, bar, chairs, tables, dartboard, customers.

And a fireplace in the middle of the room... a fireplace built into a pillar right bang in the middle of the room, didn't look as if it had hosted a fire for a very long time, a dim light in the ceiling revealing a grate containing old ash, cold ash, with a ledge above, upon which looked to be a framed photograph. From Adrian's vantage point, no detail of this could be ascertained.

That was about it.

'What have they got on.'

'Have a look.'

Adrian rather liked real ale, hence his affection for Wetherspoons.

'Have they got any ales on?' Without waiting for a response, he perused the pumps.

'Excellent, I'll have a "Hobgoblin".'

'Good choice... I'll have the same... mind; the service in here can be shocking.'

Blake then turned and directed a question to an old man, sitting alone, at a table, closest to the bar, 'Maurice, is Mr Scales in charge tonight?'

The old man, wrinkled but bright-eyed, peered across at the new arrivals.

'You know that Mr Scales is always in charge, young Blake.'

Adrian heard a scuffling noise from somewhere, just at the word 'Blake'... there was movement behind the bar. On closer inspection, he noted that, to the left, the standing room behind the counter extended into a passageway leading off into some dark (or, more accurately, darker) space. It was from this cave that the scuffling noise had emanated.

'It's a bit dark in here, isn't it?' Thought it worthwhile to pass the obvious to his host.

'Good... it means that no-one will know we're over-dressed.'

A shadow formed in the cave, created by some back-lighting. The barman emerged into the light, and what a sight! Overall initial impression was very tall, detail hard to distinguish at this stage, insufficient illumination, and the figure was too far away. As it approached, resolution improved... certainly tall, wearing a polo-necked top of some description, very tight around the throat, almost like a dog-collar... but no vicar was this. Thin, very, very thin, very long, long was a good word, thought Adrian. Even the head was long, only just enough room for a face in such a very thin head, all squeezed in. A face viewed as a reflection in a distorting mirror in the fairground.

'Evening, Mr Roberts.'

Voice was kind of a gurgle, sounded like it was coming out of water. If a fish could talk, this might well have been how it sounded.

'Evening, Mr Scales.'

The erstwhile governor of the establishment appeared to move in a most unusual way. Whereas most humans sort of "bob" forward, first one foot and then the other placed on the ground causing a natural rocking motion, left to right... not so with Mr Scales. Mr Scales' motion was as smooth as that of a ghost, a sliding approach, hardly any extraneous movement at all, a translation, the moving of a piece on a chessboard. There was no hair on Mr Scales, hardly a nose to speak of, not enough room for a nose, the eyes were too big, and the face too thin. Eyes were half the face... very round, the only Scales features that weren't thin. The pupils were thin within the circles, though, thin and black, fine, upstanding pupils. Skin on the face appeared to be brown, or was it just the light, or the lack of it... and with a strange sheen that reminded Adrian of something that he couldn't quite remember.

'I see that you have a companion.'

'I do, indeed, Mr Scales... this is Adrian, a good friend and colleague, Adrian, this is Mr Scales.'

Mr Scales nodded, stiffly.

Adrian put out a hand to be shaken, as you would, but there was no hand from Mr Scales. Both of Mr Scales' hands were kept out of sight below the counter.

'What can I get you, gentlemen?'

'Two "Hobgoblins," I think.'

Nothing seemed to happen at this point. Mr Scales did not walk towards the pump, armed with pint glasses in the conventional way. Instead, he remained exactly where he was, arms and hands invisible. Adrian stared at him because, on top of all of the strange things about Mr Scales, there was another something that he couldn't quite put his finger on.

'Cheers!'

Blake pushed a pint of beer into his stomach. He responded as you would by grabbing it with his right hand, noticing, at the same time, that a similar pint was held in Blake's left hand.

'Where did that come from?'

'Where do you think?'

He wasn't blinking... Scales wasn't blinking! That was it! People blinked, but Mr Scales wasn't blinking.

'Come on, I'll introduce you to some of the regulars.' Blake grabbed his arm and pulled him away from the bar.

'Enjoy your night, gents,' whispered Mr Scales, sliding off back to his cave.

'Adrian, this is Alan. Alan is here every night, a true regular, ain't that right, Alan?'

That statement was manifestly not true... even the "Dark Horse" wasn't here every night... but the mischievous comment did not register unduly with Adrian because, at this stage, Adrian did not know. He merely smiled at Alan, slumped in his seat, alone at his table, nursing a half-empty glass of something in front of him, might have been whisky. Alan gurned back at him, no teeth visible, or maybe they were there, just very black, hard to see in this light... leathery face, an antique face, but probably looked older than he was, these alcoholics always looked older than they were. Adrian noted that the cardigan had seen better years, various holes and stains betraying a life well-lived.

'Evening Alan, nice to meet you.' A fraternal hand was

extended, Alan's own hand remained hidden, somewhere behind the table, seemed to be a theme developing here.

'Alan had cancer earlier this year, didn't you, Alan. Came as a hell of a shock.'

Alan nodded toothlessly.

This seemed an odd and inappropriate way to initiate the introduction. What to say in response, if anything? Adrian was never at his best in such situations.

'Glad that you're still with us.' He muttered.

At this, Blake chuckled rather inconsiderately, Alan's face breaking into a cracked smile...

'Come on, I'll introduce you to Ben.'

Once again, Adrian was hauled away... he hadn't even yet had a chance to take a sip.

At the next table, and again alone, was seated a much younger man.

'This is Ben.'

'Pleased to meet you,' said Ben, exhibiting the slightest of cockney in his delivery, face swarthy, handsome, and dressed in leather, head-to-foot. Adrian spotted the crash-helmet perched on the bench nearby and decided to use this observation to break the ice.

'Looks like you are into biking.'

There was that smile again, albeit this time accompanied by a full set of teeth. Ben then rose from his seat via a series of contortions, table taking the strain. Even so, the movement was clearly causing a great deal of discomfort.

'Are you OK?' For the first time Adrian noticed the scar on the boy's forehead, for boy, he was, maybe eighteen. Eyes were drawn to that scar, a significant scar, led from the centre of the forehead right across the top of the face, turning right and finally disappearing behind the hairline. Above this point of transition, a bare patch of skin roared out from the scalp, almost square, as if the hair had been cut away. Not so handsome now, as maybe he once was.

'Looks like you've been in the wars,' said Adrian, making conversation on the back of nerves, saying anything that came into his head.

'Ben was in a very serious accident, weren't you, Ben?' Blake declared.

Ben nodded, 'Very serious it was... too right.'

'Someone died,' added Blake.

'God... that's really bad... must be difficult to get over that. I suppose you can't really ever get over it.'

'Can't get over someone dying... sorry, I didn't catch your name,' Ben extended his head forward, as if struggling to hear, brought the injuries even closer, very in-your-face.

'Sorry, my fault, Ben... this is Adrian. He... works with me at "Simkins."'

Ben nodded and collapsed back into his chair, 'Think I'll have one more before I..., think I'll have one more, can I get you two gentleman a drink?'

Adrian then realised that he still hadn't taken a sip from his pint... glancing at his companion's glass, he observed that, by contrast, half of the brown liquid had been consumed. Before he could respond to Ben's offer (no, obviously), Blake chipped in, 'Thanks, but I want to introduce Adrian to the Palmers.'

The Palmers were a middle-aged couple in matching white and grey sweaters, Mr Palmer bespectacled, frames held together with slices of masking tape, Mrs Palmer displaying what looked like a birthmark covering most of her left cheek.

They had suffered a house fire about a year ago.

'They lost their cat in the fire,' Blake elaborated grimly.

The Palmers were at a table two along from Ben the motorcyclist (intervening table being unoccupied). Adrian reasoned that the almost-full pint belonged to Mr P and the gin-and-tonic looking drink, his wife... this assumption crushed when the old boy reached for the smaller glass. By this point, he was feeling like an extra in a horror movie and so began to look around attempting to appear normal, various other oddities seated on the benches on the other side of the bar huddled around tables, a low murmur of conversation resembling the buzzing drone of a gathering of bees.

My God that looks like Gerry!

Adrian squinted in the dim light... it *was* Gerry, Gerry, on his own at a table in the corner, Gerry eating crisps. Rotund and flat-headed, the latter impression arising from a curious hairstyle.

'Gerry!' The greeting was delivered with a sense of elation... at last some manifestation of familiarity. Everyone stopped talking and looked towards the source of the noise. Gerry occasionally played golf at the "Regency" course just outside Stedford, Adrian also occasionally played golf there... occasionally they found themselves there at the same time... neither were members, too expensive, but you could get a good deal for a single round (not at weekends), and so their paths had crossed a few times. Hardly a bosom buddy was Gerry, but any port in a storm.

'Well, well, Adrian... I never thought I'd see you in the "Horse", what the hell are you doing here... does Claire know you're out?'

The words were uttered at an annoyingly high volume, and so the natives could tune in, isolated chuckles breaking out around the bar. Adrian blushed, but no-one would have been able to see, it was too dark. He patted his acquaintance on the right shoulder... Gerry was wearing what looked like an old gardening jumper, not his usual style; he was generally well-turned out. Meanwhile, Blake was somewhat wrong-footed by this grand meeting. He didn't recognise "Gerry", thought he knew everyone that drank in the "Horse"... didn't recognise this "Gerry". Annoyingly, Adrian had already left his side and taken up a station next to Gerry's table and was offering this stranger a drink.

'Can I get you a drink, Gerry?'

'Don't think so... I'd better get away shortly. I'll get into trouble with the missus.'

Happily, by this stage, the "Horse's" occupants had returned to their own business, attention diverted, Adrian, for the first time since he had walked through the door, began to relax, though this resurgence was tempered by the knowledge that ordinary Gerry was about to leave.

'Sure you can't stay for another?' Adrian became conscious of the presence of Blake, who had silently followed him across the floor and was now standing very close by.

'No, gotta go. You can have my seat.'

'Excellent... by the way, I'm Blake.' Said Blake.

'Nice to meet you, Blake, anyway gotta go.'

And off he went, Blake and Adrian replacing him at the table. Nothing was said for a minute or maybe several... rapid sips being taken from pints. Adrian had some catching up to do.

'What do you make of the... oogh, that hurt.'

Blake's conversation starter cut off before it saw the full light of day.

'Everything OK?'

'Indigestion... bloody ropey beer!' Chest melodramatically rubbed.

'Should be used to it by now... as I was saying, what do you make of the place?'

'Looks like most of the customers have had plenty of bad luck.'

'That's life. Who was Gerry?'

'Just a guy I know from the golf club'... That sounded good.

'Didn't know you played golf.'

'Don't have a lot of time.'

'I know the feeling. I couldn't play in the last Philips Medal at my course 'cos of a blasted meeting... reckoned I had a good chance as well this year... what's your handicap?'

Adrian's face contracted Riga Mortis at this point, but Lord be praised, he was rescued by the reappearance of Mr Scales, gliding in from some infernal haven.

'Sorry all, we have to close.'

Groans of disappointment filled the dank air.

'Not again!' Came the cry from an old codger, sitting three tables down from Blake and Adrian.

'Not my fault, you know the rules... the wind has changed, definitely coming from the North. You'll all have to go.'

Old codger continued to protest.

'Can't we finish our drinks?'

'You know the rules of the "Dark Horse", off you go.'

'Sorry, Adrian, we have to leave, drink up... bugger, this indigestion is killing me.'

'What's this bollocks about the wind coming from the North?'

'Ooogh... no time to explain, drink... actually I'll leave this.'

'I'm not guzzling this either... What's going on?'

Everyone was rising and pulling on jackets... this was a serious evacuation.

'Goodnight all, see you next time...,' Mr Scales gurgled very loudly, and effectively, the strange mumble echoing around the bar, audible above the scraping of chairs and general hubbub, '... I'll collect the glasses at the next opening.'

All the customers, maybe a dozen or so, left the house... pretty much all of them heading in the same direction, the direction from which Adrian and Blake had come. Adrian could make out the young motorcyclist, Ben, hobbling up the road, right leg protesting at the demands placed on it.

'Do you fancy popping into the "Poachers"?... It's still early.' Blake suggested as the figures receded into the distance.

Adrian wasn't in the mood, 'No, I think I'll head home. I've had enough excitement for one night.'

'Should have been here for Mr Scales' party piece.'

'What was that?'

'I'll tell you about it some time.'

The two began the walk home. It was a fine night, though, with a strong wind from the North, it had definitely changed direction from earlier in the evening. To Adrian's relief, their own direction of travel was now opposite to that of the regulars.

'What's that?'

'What's what?'

'That grinding sound.'

'Oh... that.' Blake nodded. 'Probably nothing.'

'It's coming from behind us, I think. Hope it's not a car crash,' Adrian prepared his body to turn around and have a look. He paused in response to a Blakean hand on his shoulder... a firm hand. 'Best not look round.'

'Why not, just seeing...'

'Best not look round.'

Blake grabbed his right arm and forced him into a march, 'Time to go home, work tomorrow.'

My, your tone has certainly changed, thought Adrian, a minute ago, you were all for more beer. The sound from behind continued to concern him, mechanical... maybe the closest parallel was that of a dustbin lorry, chewing up the waste that had just been dumped into its rear end. This odd, rumbling, grinding sound continued until they reached the end of Stable Road... then all was quiet, whatever it was, too far away now.

The two walked on, pretty much silent, it was now cold, and Adrian wanted to get home as soon as possible. Mind was starting to process the events of the night, and it wasn't going well. Impossible pub, the "Dark Horse", couldn't be there, couldn't have drunk in the "Dark Horse"... and the customers... weirdos the lot of them... except Gerry, Gerry wasn't weird, but the rest of them, cancer, house fires, crashes, how can so many people in one place have so many bad things happen to them?

Past "Simkins"... soon time to split up, Blake would turn to the right and Adrian to the left, along Jamieson Street, in opposite directions, just like going home from work.

'See you tomorrow,' Blake waved. 'Sorry, the "Horse" didn't work out. We should try again another time... bloody weather forecasts. Just can't rely on 'em.'

He was off, no chance to reply.

Adrian was on his own... time for the mind to really get going... being inside the pub seemed almost normal, the normality of the present, just take it all in. No time to realise that it was impossible... it was different now, input had been lost, now he had the freedom to be afraid. Walking quickly might help; getting home quickly would help.

Fleeting thought to call in for some chips, hadn't eaten, not a good thing but the need to get home was too strong.

'You're back early,' the greeting from Claire was less welcoming than he had expected, or maybe he was just paranoid.

'How did it go?'

'Very strange.'

She was talking about the meeting at the Business Hub.

He was thinking about the "Dark Horse".

'Bloody pub... there isn't a pub on Stable Road, is there? You know Stable Road, there isn't a pub there, is there?'

He was holding her hand in the middle of the lounge, TV whispering away in the background, 'Not that I know of... not that I'm an expert.'

'You don't have to be an expert...', voice rose just a notch,

'... you'd know if there was a pub there and there isn't, and yet... and yet... and this is so bloody impossible... me and Blake had a pint there tonight... and the customers were all freaks by the way... all had diseases or were in car crashes or house fires... except Gerry. Gerry was in there.'

'Golf club Gerry?'

'Yeh, he was in there, and then the place closed because the wind was in the wrong direction, something like that... and the landlord was...'

He was holding her hand very tightly now, and every second or so, he would clasp it even more tightly, and then release it again, building up a rhythm a little like a heartbeat, in... out... in... out. Claire was climbing into anxiety... this was new territory for her... a ranting Adrian.

'Calm down.'

'I am calm.'

Maybe he had had a few too many... but it was early, he wouldn't have had time to drink too much... and she was pretty sure he was right; there were no pubs on Stable Road.

'Have you had anything to eat?'

'Not yet; we went straight from the meeting.'

'And how was the meeting?'

'Dull as dishwater...'

Slowly, the intensity of the grip lessened as the tension eased, 'Have *you* eaten yet?'

Claire considered this a promising development... intelligent questioning.

'I have, I thought you might be home late, but I can make you something... how about a bacon sandwich?'

'Now you're talking... sorry for the rant... it's just...'

'Fine, fine,' Claire acted to quench any possible resurgence of the angst. 'No worries... I'll go and make it.'

Ninety minutes later, they were in bed, Claire lying on her side, facing away from him, Adrian bolt upright and very close to her. Following a short silence, he, once again, raised the topic of the "Dark Horse".

'You should google it... if it really exists, you'll find it on google,' she said. Adrian sank into the comfort zone and wrapped an arm about her.

'But it does exist... or at least it did... I was in there, for Christ's sake.'

He suddenly jerked up again, 'And the fireplace!'

'What about it?'

'There was smoke coming out the chimney... and no fire in the fireplace!'

'Shut up and go to sleep.'

'The fireplace!'

'Shut up and go to sleep!'

Reluctantly he went underground again... but retained the google idea... he would try that out tomorrow.

He did just that, in the office, following morning coffee.

Typed in "The Dark Horse" on his PC. There were numerous hits, but the Wikipedia entry drew his attention for no obvious reason.

search

For other uses, see **Dark Horse (disambiguation)**.

A **dark horse** *is a little-known person or thing that emerges to prominence, especially in a competition of some sort,[1] or a contestant that seems unlikely to succeed.[2]*

There were no references to a pub; he should refine the search... not now though, his project abruptly terminated by the unexpected arrival of Frank Salmon.

169

'Morning, Adrian... just wanted a quick debrief on yesterday's events.'

On the following Saturday, Adrian paid a visit to Miss Fingalstone.

Miss Fingalstone had taught Adrian at Stedford Secondary back in the day, Adrian being born and schooled in the town. He had married Claire, a local girl, and they had rented a flat for a while, quite close to the building that later became "Wetherspoons", Adrian drifting through a range of un-promising jobs. Then the position had come up at "Simkins", and they had decided to buy a house in Farely so that he could be closer to work, Claire magnanimously consenting to commute to her own workplace.

By a strange twist of fate, Miss Fingalstone had also decided to move to Farely following her retirement, buying a small semi-detached in Stable Road. They had formed a loose kind of friendship down the years, Adrian popping over now and again, sometimes for a cup of tea and a chat, sometimes to carry out some household maintenance, he serving as her go-to person for domestic emergencies.

On this occasion, Adrian was delivering a clock that she had ordered from a shop in Stedford. The intention was that the item be delivered to her house directly from the clock factory; however, due to some administrative error on the part of "Allsop's Clock's 'n Watches", the wall-clock (white, plastic, water- and fire-proof, charges include VAT and delivery) had been sent to the shop.

'That means I'll have to go across to Stedford and pick it up,' Miss Fingalstone had informed him when they had met at "Prime" newsagents a couple of weeks previously, following a detailed explanation by her of the situation.

'You should just ask them to bring it to your place... it's their mistake.'

'I should, but it's such a faff.'

'Tell you what, I'll go across and pick it up for you.'

'That's very kind of you, Adrian!'

'Don't mention it.'

Then he had forgotten all about it... not surprising considering all that had happened in the interim... until this Saturday morning when, without any reason, he had remembered it.

'I'll pop over to Stedford and pick up that clock for old Fingalstone,' he had informed Claire while they were both still in bed, but she didn't know what he was talking about, Adrian having failed to mention the original conversation with the old dear.

'What clock?'

'Tell you later.'

'Will she be in?'

'Bound to be.'

Armed with the clock in question (had been a devil of a job persuading "Allsop's" to release it, but he had succeeded, following application of his most persuasive manner), Adrian opened Miss Fingalstone's garden gate, strode down the short path and knocked on Miss Fingalstone's door (needed to place the clock, in its bespoke box, on the ground in order to do so), no sign of Miss Fingalstone. He knocked again after a minute or two, not unduly concerned as the old lady was a little on the deaf side. Concern mounted, however, following a lack of response to the second knock.

'Ah, Adrian!'

Words came as something of a shock. Miss Fingalstone had been at the back of the house, pottering around her small rear garden, had this situation continued, she would not have heard the knocks on the door. Crisis would have escalated;

good job she had decided to come round front at the critical moment.

'Hello, Miss Fingalstone, how are you?' Old habits died hard, never called her by her first name, couldn't... in any case didn't remember what it was.

'Not bad at all, considering... come into the house.'

'I've got the clock for you... sorry I hadn't brought it round sooner.'

'Not at all. It's very kind of you to pick it up for me.'

A concrete path circled the house, making her journey from the back garden to the front door easier than it might have been... arthritis in the hip had gotten worse over the past year, accentuating an old limp. A short woman, maybe only five feet, had gotten smaller since the form-three days... maybe people do shrink as they get older... white hair, slight stoop to add to the limp, God knows how old she was, she had always been old, now she was older than that. Right cheek hosted a mole, inspiring the nickname "Molly" in the Stedford Secondary lexicon... Adrian now smiling at the memory.

Miss Fingalstone pushed at the front door and hobbled inside the house, Adrian following.

'Put the clock down, looks heavy... I'll make us both a cup of tea.'

The old bird led the way through a small hallway into the front room. He dumped his load on the floor and flexed his arms.

'It was heavy, wasn't it?'

'Not really.'

'Sit yourself down.'

A comfortable, indeed a cozy room was the front room of Miss Fingalstone, sparsely furnished, but how many chairs do you need when there is only one of you? Never married to Adrian's knowledge though there were photographs of people, maybe friends or family, all over the place, on the dresser against the wall next to the window, on the shelf above the fireplace, and in the cabinet to Adrian's left as he entered the room. Black-and-white most of them... though the one in the centre of the fireplace shelf was in colour... a young blond-haired man with an engaging smile and wearing what might have been a uniform of some description. Who was he, family member or a past sweetheart?

The old lady slipped off a green cardigan and shuffled off into the kitchen. Meanwhile, Adrian made himself at home in a too-comfortable armchair next to a low table that was home to a fish tank. The ex-schoolteacher kept fish, two of them, goldfish in a tank, looked quite exotic but certainly goldfish, they had names, Iris and Larry. Miss Fingalstone was able to tell them apart, no problem, Adrian never could.

'Would you like me to put the clock up for you?' He shouted after her, had to shout very loudly to overcome the deafness.

'No... no, I may be decrepit, but I can do that. I have a set of steps somewhere,' she shouted back at him, voice echoey.

Adrian found this slightly alarming, 'I'm not sure that you should be climbing up steps...' He almost added, '... at your age' but decided against it.

'Get away with you!' Her accent was slightly west-country, maybe Bristolian.

'How are the fish doing?'

'Fine, Iris is full of beans at the moment.' Conversation continued at high volume due to Miss F's remote location. As the sole human in the lounge, Adrian glanced across at the creatures. Both were swimming in contra-rotating circles about halfway up... or down in the tank, depending on your perspective... gulping away... which one was bloody Iris? And how does a fish demonstrate that it is full of beans?

'That's the kettle boiling. I'll bring the tea out... do you want a biscuit?'

'That sounds good... I don't want to put you out, Miss

Fingalstone.'

'Not at all, I've got some "Rich Tea".'

The rattle of a tray preceded the re-appearance of Miss Fingalstone.

'I'll take that,' said Adrian, determined to be helpful.

'No, no, I'm not an invalid,' replied the invalid. 'I'll put it down over here, now... that's done.'

She poured herself a cup and selected a biscuit before dropping heavily into a red armchair.

'So, Adrian, how are things with you?'

'Good, very good... how about you?'

Adrian rose from his seat to help himself.

'Awfully sorry, excuse my manners.'

'Not at all,' he poured from the pot. It weighed a ton... the old dear was stronger than she looked. Having filled a fragile-looking cup and sequestered his own biscuit, he carefully resumed his position.

'So how are you... are you sure that you don't want me to put the clock up?'

'No, I'll manage. I haven't decided where to put it yet.'

They both sipped, Adrian feeling slightly ridiculous for no reason.

'Looks like Iris and Larry are pleased to see you... they can't take their eyes off you.'

'So I see.' It would be an exaggeration to say that he felt the eyes of the fish burning into his soul... but they did seem to be now looking at him, even pausing the mindless perambulation of their tiny pool to better focus on the new human.

'How's work?'

'Good, I might be in for a promotion...' At that moment, and following the completion of his first biscuit, Adrian decided to ask a very strange question... or maybe not a question, not a real direct question, more a line of enquiry.

'That pub down the road... Is it any good?'

'What pub? I'm no expert on pubs, Adrian, you know me.'
Miss Fingalstone plucked another biscuit from the plate
and collapsed back into her chair.

'The "Dark Horse".'

These words arrived as she was taking her first bite, and
while not exactly causing a choke, they did lead to a pause in
the chewing.

'The "Dark Horse"?'

'Yes.'

'Why do you ask?'

Now he had to think quickly.

'Just fancied a pint on the way home, wondered whether I
might pop in... on the way home... if it is still there' (he didn't
say the last five words).

'The "Dark Horse"... well, well.' Miss Fingalstone applied
her dentures to the immediate task of demolishing a second
biscuit.

'Well?'

'Well, what?'

Adrian was chomping at the bit, if not the biscuit, for some
progress in these increasingly gnomic exchanges, 'Just
wondered if you knew what the place was like.'

The old trouper scrambled out of her seat and made for
the window, 'Tell me about the promotion... sounds exciting.'

Adrian bit his lower lip; this was excruciating. Ask a simple
question, and then all this nonsense... What game was she
playing? He decided to play hardball.

'I'll tell you about the promotion after you tell me about
the pub.'

She then proceeded to lift the handle to open the window.
There followed a period of silence as she seemed to smell the
air drifting into the room.

'Probably a good time to visit.'

'What's that supposed to mean?'

'Looks like the wind is...'

Halfway through the sentence, Adrian got very excited, couldn't help finishing it.

'Don't tell me... wind is from the South?'

The words were uttered as he rose from his remarkably comfortable chair... wanted to also look out of the window, to maybe see what she could see. There they stood, both staring out of the window into the old girl's garden, grass appeared recently cut though there wasn't enough growth this time of year to warrant deployment of the mower. Flowerbeds were all empty.

'The "Horse" should be open.'

That did not come from Miss F... not at all, not her voice at all, and it didn't come from where she was standing. Adrian's feet began to tingle; something was up. Voice was of a deep timbre, slightly distorted as if emanating from a cupboard or dungeon or cave or some-place like any of those places.

'What did you say?'

'I didn't say anything,' said Miss Fingalstone.

'Didn't you hear it...' I thought someone said, 'The "Horse" should be open.'

He swung round, half expecting to see someone else, but of course, there wasn't anyone; there couldn't be anyone else. Eyes drawn to the fish tank, Iris and Larry doing their thing. Hard to see precisely from where Adrian was standing but looked like one of the creatures had his or her body fully side on to him, a proper broadside, hovering in mid-water, tiny fins working to hold position rather like a helicopter, eyes forever unblinking. The room was very quiet now except for the slight hummering from the bubbles of the aerating device in the tank.

'You must have imagined it. I didn't hear anything.'

'Could have sworn...'

Body was tense... no fooling the body, knew that something was not right. Miss Fingalstone looked at him, really looked at him, 'Seems like you know all you need to know.'

That was a strange thing to say... What did that mean?

'Look at the fish, they're certainly full of beans now, must be all this talk about the "Dark Horse".' Another piece of nonsense talk.

Glancing at the tank, Iris and Larry were back in motion, round and round in circles, meeting each other twice every revolution. He decided then that he should leave, 'I should probably go, Miss Fingalstone. If you have any issues with the clock, just get in touch.'

'I don't think that will be necessary, Adrian... thanks for bringing it over.'

He drained the last drops of tea and stood up.

'I will pop into the pub... try not to get the rolling pin off Claire!'

'Ah, Claire. How is she doing?'

Blast, didn't want to get into a conversation about Claire... just wanted to get out.

'Fine, fine... I'll see you next time, Miss Fingalstone... and if you want any help with the clock, just give me a bell!'

'I'll see you out.'

Huge sigh when he hit the road... he was in need of a pint. Quick glance at the watch reinforced the sensation from the stomach. Both said lunchtime. Did the "Horse" serve food? Hadn't seen any evidence during the first visit, no menus on the tables, no boards on the walls, no empty plates or discarded napkins. No humming from kitchen extractor fans or enticing smells.

No harm in finding out.

Adrian walked past a spire-less church on the right, St.

John's, a sign that he was getting close to where the "Dark Horse" had been the last time... the fact that it hadn't been there the time before, or the one before that, etc., etc. was neither here nor there. Stomach was churning now, not knowing whether a building would be where it was on the last visit. Hadn't been in the neighborhood of the "Horse" thus far on this trip... no opportunity to see if it was there or not, having taken the bus from Stedford, route via Albion Lane and then the top end of Stable Road, close to the "Simkins" building. This brought him close to Fingalstone's place; therefore, hadn't passed where the pub should be... So would it be?

Ten more yards, past the bike shop... that was here, of course it was, it had been here since 1975, "Wright's Bikes... Established 1975"... said so above the long windows, no reason to doubt it... and then, one more block along, the gap site, or would it be the "Dark Horse"?

Heart was racing as he peered around the red brick walls of the Victorian house, next door to the... maybe...

There it was... the square building with its pointed red roof and its red walls and red curtains and smoke coming out of its offset chimney. Adrian didn't know whether to laugh or cry. Now that the pub was there, and there was an inside to go into, he had to go into it, just had to. Inside the place, it was much as before, the same old semi-familiar faces. The guy who had had the bike accident was there, and the Palmers, all in the usual seats, and the fireplace was dead, just as before.

Mr Scales stood behind the bar.

'Good afternoon, sir,' Came the familiar gurgle. 'Nice to see you again.'

'Hello.' No sign of food anywhere... hard for a pub to survive these days if it didn't serve food, hard for a pub to survive these days if the wind was coming from the North. Adrian walked to the bar... looked around, and presented a nervous smile to the regulars, no-one acknowledged him. Maybe they didn't remember that they had seen him before. He was just about to ask Mr Scales for a menu when his eyes alighted on a familiar face seated at the end of the bar.

Looked like Blake. Blake on his own on a bar-stool.

'Hello, Blake!'

Blake twisted on his seat. It was definitely Blake.

'Well, you've come back!'

'Actually, I was hoping to get some food. I've just come from Miss Fingalstone's place, my old teacher, delivered a clock for her.'

He walked towards the figure on the stool, first thought was that Blake didn't look too great, appeared paler than normal, or maybe it was the light, must be the light. Hard to tell.

'We don't serve food, I'm afraid,' gurgled Mr Scales. 'That is, except for nuts and crisps.'

'In that case, I'll have a pint of "Hobgoblin"... can I get you one, Blake? I see you have an empty glass?'

'I'm afraid the "Hobgoblin" is off... we rotate our beers, we have "Pedigree", "Pendle Witches' Brew"...'

'I'll have that.'

'Pendle?'

'Yes... One for you, Blake?'

'Thanks.'

Almost exactly thirty seconds later, Adrian felt something being pushed into his stomach, eyes swung down to see the pint glass in his hand... just like last time. A quick glance at Blake confirmed that he, too, had a pint in his hand.

'How are you doing?' Adrian leant on the bar next to Blake super casually, doing his best to look as if he belonged.

'Not great. Went for a walk this morning and felt a pain in my chest.' He brought a hand up and placed it over his heart.

A ringtone rang out across the bar. 'Sorry,' said Adrian,

plucking his phone from the inside pocket of his jacket. Slightly embarrassing... always got embarrassed when this sort of thing happened. Did the background mumble of conversation grow ever-so-slightly louder at the sound... a heightened mumble of disapproval? The mobile's screen glowed brightly in the near dark of the "Horse". The call was from the wife.

'Hello, Claire. What's up? Really sorry about this, Blake,' he smiled weakly, Blake simply watching in a disinterested fashion. There was a strange sound from the other end of the line, a kind of strangled cough... didn't sound good. 'Are you OK?'

'Where are you?'

Bugger, should he lie, or should he lie?

'Why do you ask?'

'I think you should come home.'

'Why, what's happened?'

Embarrassment swept away in a second... didn't like the sound of this at all.

'Are you sure you're OK?'

'Who are you talking to?... I heard you talking to someone.'

'OK, I ran into Blake on the way home from Miss F's. He dragged me into the pub for a drink, just the one.'

There was merely the sound of breathing for a while... quite a while, followed by another cough.

'Look, Adrian, this is in very bad taste... are you drunk... you can't be. The pubs have only just opened.'

Embarrassment had been replaced first by panic, now by confusion... supplemented by panic.

'What the f... hell are you on about?'

He smiled again at Blake, 'Sorry about this.'

'You should listen to what she has to say... you might learn something,' smiled Blake, a particularly crooked smile.

'What with the horrible news and all that... who told you?'

To Adrian's ears, Claire sounded slightly hysterical.

'Who told me what... what are you talking about?'

'Blake's heart attack.'

'Heart attack... it's just indigestion.'

'That's just heartless... cruel. I'm surprised at you.'

'Look... who told you that he had a heart attack?'

'John Semple.'

John Semple was a family friend of some years' standing, also knew the Roberts.

'John was walking past the house and saw the ambulance. He overheard the paramedics... nothing more they could do; that's what he heard them say. I saw him at the newsagents; he was still white as a sheet.'

There were other words, but they were not received.

'What did she want?' Asked Blake, knowing, of course, exactly what she wanted.

'Alan had cancer earlier this year, didn't you, Alan. Came as a hell of a shock.'

'Ben was in a very serious accident, weren't you, Ben?' Blake declared.

Ben nodded, 'Very serious it was... too right.'

'Someone died,' added Blake.

The Palmers were a middle-aged couple in matching white and grey sweaters, Mr Palmer bespectacled, frames held together with slices of masking tape, Mrs Palmer displaying what looked like a birthmark covering most of her left cheek.

They had suffered a house fire about a year ago.

Two options were open to Adrian, faint or flight. Suddenly he was awash with energy, and so he decided to run for it... all the way home with the voices sounding inside of his head, though with decreasing volume.

'Not great. Went for a walk this morning and felt this pain in my chest.'

It felt late, but it was still only early afternoon by the time he pretty much crashed through the front door of the house. He needed to explain everything to Claire. A trouble shared is a trouble doubled; that was it. She was waiting for him in the front room.

'God, am I pleased to see you!' He wheezed... had a touch of asthma, didn't bother him most of the time, but the run home was too much for the lungs.

'What the hell is going on, Adrian?'

'Not sure... I was speaking with Blake in the pub... he was standing next to me, I swear!'

He collapsed into a chair, all the senses ringing away like bells in a tower, needed to calm down, heart was pumping like a steam engine. Anxiety swam through his body, buggering up everything. Then he started to laugh, hysteria presumably... as if he didn't have enough to worry about; now he was bloody hysterical.

'You need to calm down. I'll pour you a G&T.'

'Make it a large one.' That was probably a bad idea, but what the hell? Emergency measures now required. Sure enough, following a few sips, he could feel his body subsiding, might have been psychosomatic, but if it worked, happy days.

'Thing is, I think that they were all dead... all of the customers were dead.'

'Ben was in a very serious accident, weren't you Ben?' Blake declared.

Ben nodded, 'Very serious it was... too right.'

'All except Gerry... Gerry was alive, is alive.'

'And you, you were alive,' added Claire.

'And me, yes... I'll get another drink, do you want one?'

'Better not.'

'Someone died,' added Blake.

'But everyone else is dead... Blake is dead, but I was talking to the f... to him, I was TALKING to him, we were drinking together.'

Claire sank into a chair. Maybe she could have just one...

At four o'clock, they both decided, at the same time, to go to bed, the gin bottle having run dry. Up to the marital bedroom, it was, helping each other up the stairs... minimum preparation required, needed to get into the soft heaven as quickly as possible. Normally, Adrian would perform a regulation sweep of the house before bedtime, check that the doors were locked, that sort of thing... but this was the middle of the afternoon, and he was a bit pissed, and so he didn't bother. As he rose slowly towards his destination, he vowed to continue the discussion concerning the afternoon's events once they were both in bed, but fatigue and intoxication overtook him rapidly after home-base was achieved. Next to him, touching him, Claire remained upright, too agitated to contemplate sleep, yet silent, thoughtful.

The voices welcomed him to the dark mind.

'Alan had cancer earlier this year, didn't you, Alan. Came as a hell of a shock.'

Next morning, they both had hangovers. Together, in bed and in torment, they bathed in the sea of regret. It was nine o'clock on a Sunday morning. Claire was suffering somewhat more than her partner, being less familiar with the experience, refusing to emerge from the womb of the bed while Adrian lay on his back, staring at a ceiling that was still rotating slightly. Inside the throbbing head was the echo of a dream. He had definitely been dreaming... he could recall that he had had a dream, just not what the dream was about. He didn't feel bad about his dream, so it had probably been a good dream, he wished that he could remember it, but despite his best efforts, he couldn't.

'We should get up.'

'I don't want to,' mumbled the recumbent wife.

'OK... it's only nine o'clock. We don't normally get up this early on a Sunday.'

So, they lay there for a while, Claire dozing and Adrian super-awake. No discussions ensued about yesterday, hangovers being great for taking one's mind off things. At eleven, they went for it... downstairs was not that far away, but the idea from earlier in the week to go for a long and rejuvenating walk on Sunday... 'Looking forward to it,'... Claire had said in response to his suggestion, was abandoned as the full horror of seeing out the day burned into their souls.

Adrian awoke very early on the Monday, the awakening accompanied by a deadly blast of anxiety, a proper hand-grenade hurled into his bed at five o'clock. No hangover to shield him this time. Work was only four hours away. Four hours, however, was not to be sniffed at... even if he had to lay awake for four hours; that was no bad thing. Four hours was ages, and Claire was fast asleep. She would be asleep until at least six-thirty.

What would happen at work? What would Frank say? Would there be a gathering of the workers, a wake? Would Frank, tearfully, eulogise over Blake's life? Inform the congregation of the dear departed's contribution to "Simkins"? What an irreplaceable loss? A friend and colleague, taken before his time, who would be sadly missed? He wouldn't be mentioning the meeting of the dear Blake with himself; he, Adrian, in the "Dark Horse" an hour or so after the bastard died, would he? Certainly not.

'Will you be all right at work?' Claire asked at breakfast.

'I'll be all right, got to bite the bullet.'

She gave him a kiss to send him on his way.

As it transpired, there was to be no Churchillian oration from Frank Salmon, no flowers or cards piled in tribute, outside the entrance to "Simkins", no marking of the sad loss of Blake Roberts. Just work. Words were exchanged between Adrian and some colleagues... everyone he met, and that wasn't so many, had already heard the news.

'Terrible about Blake, wasn't it?'

'How old was he, couldn't have been that old, must have been under fifty, what sort of age is that, eh?'

Frank did pop into Adrian's office after lunch... weak smile... looked quite pale. Maybe the old git was feeling it.

'I know you were good friends, Adrian... my commiserations.'

Not exactly, thought Adrian, but he merely smiled in return, 'Very bad news, Frank.'

'The funeral will be on Friday, Lorna's sister phoned this morning; she seems to be doing all the donkey-work. Lorna is holding up as well as to be expected.'

Frank continued to smile humourlessly.

'I'm going along, will you?'

'Yes, I will.'

'Good, good, I'll send out a general e-mail to the rest of the staff... thought I'd tell you first... in person.'

'Thank you, Frank.'

Adrian breathed a sigh of relief at the closing of the door, Frank's footsteps echoing away down the corridor like a retreating army. That meant that he, Adrian, was now safe.

Friday was quite soon, clearly not too many people had died in the neighbourhood recently, no queue for the undertakers to manage. Pushing the subject of death to the back of his mind, he returned to his duties, sorting out the paperwork for the new cleaner, due to start next week, a task which took most of the morning. Then lunch (popped out to a local sandwich shop and ate the goods in a tiny "park" nearby. Just a strip of green, but the council had ennobled it as "Regent Park"), afternoon was spent on HR spreadsheets that sedated him nicely. Having gotten through the day relatively unscathed, Adrian headed for home. Odd, he had barely thought about the "Dark Horse" encounter with Blake all day; the mind had processed it, decided that it could not possibly have happened, and thrown it in the trash. That evening he slept soundly, alcohol-free. Just before he and Claire turned over, he asked the question.

'Do you want to come to the funeral on Friday?'

'I don't think so. I don't like funerals... they're so depressing.'

Adrian took a smile to the land of sleep.

He made his own way, by foot, to the church on the appointed day, straight from work, route taking him past old Fingalstone's place. The event was scheduled for ten, and so he had put on his funeral suit at home... that would mean he would be stuck with it all day, but the funeral suit and work suit were similar enough... and he could discard the jacket after "the event", that way he wouldn't look too much like an undertaker. As it happened, the venue was St. John's, close to the dreaded "Horse" and so he had been gifted the opportunity to see if that damned pub was there. He decided to do so, overshooting the church for a few blocks to check. *En route* he noted the wind direction, coming from the North... and so he predicted that he wouldn't see that brick slaughterhouse with its impossible smoking chimney. He was proven correct in his prediction. No sign of the "Horse", merely the regulation waste-plot full of dustbins and weeds, Adrian simply turned on his heels and returned to the church, accepting the insanity of the situation without question. Maybe this was how cavemen had thought about the moon and the stars, and fire... these were all impossible things but were there to see every day and night, and so had to be accepted.

Frank Salmon arrived at the church at exactly the same time as he did, resplendent in his funeral-best, for the first time wearing a suit that appeared to fit. The two moved forward toward the entrance rather like a couple shortly to be pronounced man and wife.

'Good of you to come, Adrian.'

'Had to be here.'

'Good show!'

There were words written into the ground in a kind of tablet, immediately in front of the great door of St. John's; in great golden lettering, a quotation, Adrian paused to read.

But he who kisses the joy as it flies
Lives in eternity's sun rise.

'How beautiful.' Sounded corny, but he couldn't help it.

'William Blake, I think,' replied Frank.

They were greeted by the vicar just inside the porch. Adrian knew him vaguely as an occasional attendee at the golf club. He pretended that they were best buddies, just seemed the right thing to do.

'Hello Ray, good to see you.'

Ray was a small, round piece of work, Friar Tuck in black with a shock of white hair, face looked middle-aged, but the hair was out-of-place, face of a fifty-year-old, hair of an eighty-year-old, rosy cheeks, looked like he was fond of the hard stuff.

'Ah... it's Alan, isn't it? I've seen you at the golf club a few times, can't get there as often as I would like, these days.'

'Adrian.'

'Ah... of course, Adrian, and this is?'

'Frank Salmon, from "Simkins".'

'You are both welcome to St. John's.'

Inside, Adrian looked around, and there were several familiar faces... including a decent turn-out from work. Frank sat down in a pew on the back row, having spotted someone that he knew, someone more important than Adrian, so now he would be on his own as he walked forward down the central aisle of the church. Didn't want to get to the front of the rows of seats; that would be where Lorna would be sitting, probably crying, didn't much want to get involved with that. Might be other family there, best let them get on with it. There was a seat vacant on the left, and he decided to go for it, on the next seat along sat a total stranger... large woman with an oversized hat staring straight ahead at the altar. Didn't look like she wanted to talk to anyone, and that suited Adrian just fine. He could park here and go through the motions without any communication with his fellow mourners. He would mouth the words to the hymns, didn't want to make a fool of himself by singing out of tune. Glancing around from his safe perch, he saw, across the divide of the aisle and one row in front none other than Mr Haddock! Dressed in appropriately sombre attire, he looked to be chatting animatedly to a young woman sitting in the next seat... maybe his daughter, thought Adrian... though he hadn't run into her in the fish shop.

The church was modestly sized, as churches go, just the basics, a nave, choir, two small transepts, no tower... but it was cool and calm as churches often are, and so, consequently Adrian began to relax. Didn't go into churches very often, hardly at all, not being a believer, just for funerals and weddings, like most people. Had been in a few cathedrals... tourist attractions... in his time, Ely, York, but very few bog-standard churches.

Then he saw the coffin... too busy looking around the place up to that point to notice the main body of the proceedings... the sight of the casket surprised him, so that was what all these people have come to see... the coffin of Blake Roberts. Made everything cold... it had all been going so well until he had noticed the casket, and inside the box would be the mortal remains of Blake, and that thought made him feel not so great. But then, feeling not-so-great at funerals was how you were supposed to feel, and so that was OK. Such random thoughts were interrupted by the arrival of the Vicar in all his throat-clearing glory. Silence broke out in the congregation... except for Mr Haddock, who continued to chat to his young companion... the fishmonger's voice echoing round the otherwise quiet space until he realised that he was the only one still talking. Seemed odd that Haddock was present; from the encounter in the chippy it didn't seem that he and Blake were especially close.

Then it was truly silent in St. John's.

Ray the Vicar looked around at the crowd, smiling beatifically, and then began to speak.

'It's good to see so many people here today, to celebrate the life and to mourn the passing of our friend... Blake.'

Good start, thought Adrian, at the last funeral he had attended, the Priest had got the name of the deceased wrong. Attention though, soon drifted away from Ray's eulogy... it was the stereotypical monotone that did it, a kind of word-dirge that eagerly became background church musak, absorbed by the pillars and screens of the building. Periodically, Adrian tuned in to the proceedings... 'A proud employee of "Simkins"'...

Who was Simkin or Simkins? Adrian had no idea. These

days, "Simkins" was a firm of couriers, maybe the first Simkin was an old fellow with a horse and cart, maybe he collected dead bodies, 'bring out your dead!' That kind of caper. Frank would know, might be a useful conversation starter if he ever needed it.

'Well Frank, I've been thinking... who the hell was Simkin?'

Time for the first hymn, and everyone had to stand up as the opening organ notes burst forth, one or two thus-far contained coughs breaking out in sympathy. "Jerusalem", of course, Adrian mouthing furiously to avoid embarrassment (his). As is always the case in such situations, one voice rose above the general cacophony of sharps and flats, a perfect tone, Adrian confidently associated it with Mr Haddock, and following a glance at the fishmonger, the lip movements confirmed him as the source. More eulogies... Frank Salmon spoke well, as did some chap who was a friend of the family but not known to Adrian. Lorna was out of sight beyond a sea of heads, but she would definitely be crying by now; Adrian was sure of that. One more hymn, "Oh Lord and Father of Mankind", and it was pretty much over, time for the internment. Adrian decided not to stay for that... he wasn't feeling too well by this point, had a headache. Should probably have gone to offer commiserations to Lorna but decided not to do that either... wasn't really his scene. Following a cursory handshake with Ray, he found himself walking out of the church with Frank. As they stepped across the words of William Blake, Adrian concluded that he should break the silence that had accompanied them down the aisle.

'I thought you spoke well.'

'Thanks... look, Adrian, maybe this isn't the time but, not to beat around the bush, having er... lost Blake, obviously, this puts a different complexion on the ah... promotion that you were both up for.'

He was right, this wasn't the time. Adrian didn't respond.

'Clearly, you are the... now... you are the man in the hot-seat.'

Adrian just kept on walking, head staring at the ground... they were now close to the front gate of the churchyard, behind and to the left, many of the mourners had gathered at the grave-to-be. Blake Roberts was about to be interred, and here was Frank, blabbering about promotions. You couldn't make it up.

'We've decided... it's been decided that we should have some kind of interview... interview may not be the right word, maybe a meeting, just to ah... tick the boxes, if you get my meaning.'

Suddenly, Adrian began to take notice.

'I seem to remember that no interviews were in the plan for this.'

A thought flashed through Frank's mind, the thought that maybe Adrian wasn't that dim after all... he had remembered the "no-interview" line, had picked it up, and remembered it.

'Good show! Right, change of plan, are you still on board?'

Adrian wanted to say, 'Have I any choice?'

What he actually said was, 'Of course, happy to come along.'

'Excellent, good show... it'll be next Wednesday, some members of the board will be there... I'll send you the details tomorrow... er no... Monday.'

'Wednesday, that's a bit soon.'

'Best get it out of the way. Can I give you a lift back to work? I'm parked just up the street?'

'No, I'll walk if you don't mind... won't take more than half-an-hour.'

'Understood, you were very close, time to yourself... don't rush back.'

Frank waved as he crossed the road, Adrian noting the Jag

stationed obtrusively several blocks away.

*

'How did it go?' Asked Claire that evening, as they sat together in the front room, both holding G&Ts... the wife was learning. TV was on, but neither of them was watching it.

'Funerals are funerals... interesting chat with Frank, though.'

'You're being very matter-of-fact about all of this... aren't you sad about Blake? You worked with him for years.'

Now he felt shitty.

'Course... but life goes on.'

That response made him feel even more shitty. The madness surrounding Blake's death... the "Horse" stuff, all that stuff, had been processed out of existence. Even Claire wasn't talking about it. Maybe it never really happened.

'What did Frank say?'

'Seems that I will be interviewed about the "Director of Administration" post after all, even though I'm the only candidate.'

Once again, Claire was shocked by the brutality of the words, 'Adrian... really!'

'What's up?'

'You being the "only candidate".'

'Well, s'true, isn't it? Do you want another?'

'That went down quickly.'

'It's been a stressful day.'

'I haven't finished this one.'

'Right... I'll have one more, then I'll go and fetch us some fish and chips.'

'Fish and chips again?'

'Do you have a better idea?'

'I've got some spag bol in the freezer.'

'Nah, I'll pop out to the chippy... providing old Haddock

made his way home after the funeral.'

*

The next day, Saturday, Adrian walked round to Miss Fingalstone's. She had phoned at eight-thirty... what was it about
these old-timers that made them get up so early?

'Hello, Adrian... is that Adrian?'

'It is.'

'This is Ira Fingalstone.'

'Good Morning, Miss Fingalstone.' So that was her name...
Ira.

'I hope that I haven't woken you up by telephoning at this
time of the morning.'

'Yes, you have, you old bat.' Thought Adrian.

'Not at all.'

'I'm having some problems with the clock... I don't think
there is anything to hook it to the wall... could you possibly
find time to come round and have a look?'

'I'll pop over later this morning.'

'Very kind... goodbye.'

So it was that he found himself in the vicinity of the "Dark
Horse", once again.

But the wind was blowing from the East... a cold wind.

No "Dark Horse".

It was the night before the "interview" for the job that he,
Adrian, was bound to get because he was the only candidate.
He and Claire lay together in bed, last words before sleep.

'How are you feeling about tomorrow?'

'Fine, just a formality... this time tomorrow, I will be
"Simkins" Director of Administration.'

'Don't be over-confident when you go in.'

'I won't.'

What nonsense, he, Adrian being the only candidate... what could go wrong?

'What time is it?'

'First thing.'

'Good, gets it out of the way.'

'It's not an operation.'

'Still, good to get it out of the way... phone me when you get out.'

''Course... lights out?'

'Yep.'

Next morning, the mood wasn't nearly so buoyant, the effects of the early evening G&Ts having long subsided, Adrian banging around the kitchen to little effect as Claire looked on with some concern.

'Are you OK?'

'Yes, yes, of course I'm OK... we've run out of sugar.'

'No, we haven't.'

'Yes, look, the sugar bowl is empty.'

He held out the offending bowl like a spent Olympic torch... the focus of all his rage. Claire opened one of the cupboards above the fridge and took out a full bag.

'Here you go.'

'Thanks... I didn't think we kept the new bags in that cupboard.'

'We always have done.'

He pulled the bag open... a significant amount of the contents instantly distributing themselves on the floor. 'Fuck!'

'Give it to me. I'll do it.'

The admonished child handed over the bag and watched as white crystals were skilfully poured into the bowl. He reclaimed the item and transferred two spoonfuls of the white stuff into his coffee mug.

'We should go out for a meal tonight... celebrate your promotion.'

Adrian's body visibly relaxed, 'I won't find out today, I doubt.'

'But you are the only candidate.'

That had been his line last night... now it seemed a little presumptuous.

'Let's not get ahead of ourselves.'

'We should go out anyway. I'll book a table somewhere.'

He nodded, 'I'd better go.'

'Well, good luck, phone me when you get out.'

They embraced, and he was out of the door.

River Lane, Jamieson Street.

"Simkins".

Adrian looked at his watch... perfect timing... straight in... best get it out of the way.

The boardroom was on the ground floor, he looked himself up and down, best suit, dark but worn with a brightly coloured tie to demonstrate a rebellious nature, ability to think outside of the box... no need for a coat, the air was mild outside, born on a warm westerly breeze, so no point in going along to the "Dark Horse" for a celebratory pint afterwards. Knocking assertively on the oak-effect door three times, he thought he heard a scraping of chairs from within the room... seconds passed.

'Come in!'

Grasping the handle of the door, he turned it assertively; nothing happened, the door did not open. He uttered the word 'fuck' under his breath.

'Come in!'

He wrenched the handle again, again the door did not open.

'I can't get in,' he pleaded to the door.

More scraping of chairs from within and a muffled voice uttering words that Adrian could not identify. The door opened, Adrian, off-balance, almost falling into the room. It would have been comical were it not so comical. Frank Salmon had opened the door from the inside.

'Sorry, it was locked.'

'No problem.'

'Come in.'

He followed Frank into the boardroom. Couldn't remember ever coming into this room before, he had walked past it many times, one of the two gents' toilets being at the end of the corridor, but he hadn't *actually* entered it.

'Sit down, sit down.'

The room, grandly named but modestly endowed, contained a table with associated chairs (ten) in the centre. At the far end, a cabinet offered hope of refreshment, and in the centre of the wall to the left, the same wall in which was set the entrance, hung a portrait of an old boy, just the head visible, curly white hair, red cheeks... was this Simkin, or a Simkin? Hard to pick out detail, windows shielded by blinds, lights on but underpowered, reminded Adrian of a medieval banqueting hall illuminated by a few flaming torches... or maybe a torture chamber. Frank pulled a seat away from the table, about halfway down, this being clearly where he was expected to sit.

'Sit down, Adrian... coffee?'

'Yes, please.'

Frank walked to the cabinet at the top of the room.

'How do you want it?'

'Black, two sugars.'

'I should know that by now.'

Adrian sat in the high-backed chair, as directed, before him the boardroom table stretched away into the gloom. Of the nine remaining chairs, only three were occupied (Frank's chair at the head of the table, currently vacant). Directly opposite on adjacent seats sat two men. To his right, two places down, a woman scribbled furiously into a notebook.

'Here we go, Adrian, I've brought some biscuits... ginger nuts, hope you like 'em!'

'Thanks.'

Frank placed the mug of coffee and a packet of biscuits on the table in front of him.

'Sorry about the lights... problem with the electrics apparently, been trying to get it fixed for ages.'

'No problem,' Adrian took a gulp of coffee, nerves jangling but under control.

'I should introduce the members of the board that are here. You'll know them, I'm sure, but just for the record... Alan Grimes, Finance (one of the men nodded), John Lander, Legal Services (the other man smiled, revealing a perfect set of very white teeth, very white in the dim light of the room), and last but by no means least, Alison Fisher.' (Woman continued to scribble.) Alison Fisher either didn't have a role, or maybe Frank had simply lost interest by the time he had reached her. Adrian nodded himself around the table, smiling as if happy, before draining the last of the coffee. He knew the faces of these people, had seen them around, didn't know them.

'More coffee?'

'Thanks.'

Adrian now realised that no-one else around the table was drinking coffee, but it was too late; he was committed. Off went Frank, in his undersized suit, to pour more of the vital liquid. He returned shortly and deposited a second mug within Adrian's reach.

'You're lining them up,' said John Lander, everyone chuckled.

Frank was back in his chair, home-base, and very much in control. He peered over the top of his spectacles, scanning the space... his space.

'We are still waiting for one.'

'Ah, yes, so we are,' said John... sounded vaguely Scottish, thought Adrian.

'Yes, the observer,' that was Alison, lifting her head and her hand from the journal.

'He is always late.'

That was Alan Grimes... Geordie, thought Adrian.

'Reputation for being late,' said John Lander.

There was a knock at the door.

'Come in,' shouted Frank.

'It's not locked again, is it,' enquired John.

It clearly wasn't because, presently, a just-about-recognisable Blake Roberts opened the door and walked into the room. 'Sorry, I'm late,' voice sounded as if it was coming from inside a box. Everyone laughed. Blake didn't look too good, even in the dark of the torture-boardroom, very pale, eyes were sunken pools, could hardly see them at all. He was wearing a grubby sweatshirt that had seen better days... and he'd lost weight.

'Ah Blake... about time,' said Frank.

'I got boxed in,' hissed the deceased.

'The late Blake Roberts,' added Alison.

Everyone laughed again, then Frank cleared his throat.

'We... all of us...' (he looked around the table at this point, thereby demonstrating collective responsibility), '... believe that as Blake can no longer be considered for the post of "Director of Administration", ... and knowing how close the two of you were... are, you might like him to be present at your moment of triumph... as it were.'

'Looks like you've got the gig, Adrian,' added Blake, voice now coming from somewhere outside of the room. 'You are the one still standing, congratulations!'

Everyone laughed again as Adrian wet himself.

About Atmosphere Press

Atmosphere Press is an independent, full-service publisher for excellent books in all genres and for all audiences. Learn more about what we do at atmospherepress.com.

We encourage you to check out some of Atmosphere's latest releases, which are available at Amazon.com and via order from your local bookstore:

The Friendship Quilts, a novel by June Calender

Nine Days, a novel by Judy Lannon

Shadows of Robyst, a novel by K. E. Maroudas

Dying to Live, a novel by Barbara Macpherson Reyelts

Looking for Lawson, a novel by Mark Kirby

Surrogate Colony, a novel by Boshra Rasti

Á Deux, a novel by Alexey L. Kovalev

What If It Were True, a novel by Eileen Wesel

Sunflowers Beneath the Snow, a novel by Teri M. Brown

Solitario: The Lonely One, a novel by John Manuel

The Fourth Wall, a novel by Scott Petty

Rx, a novel by Garin Cycholl

About
~ the ~
Author

David Ellis was born in
1965, near Birmingham in
the UK. He attended local
secondary Schools, first
the Queen Elizabeth Gram-
mar School and then the
Queen Elizabeth Mercian
High School. In 1984 he
enrolled at the University
of Exeter in the South-
West of England, studying chemistry and graduating in 1987.
Finding himself enthused by the subject, he completed a
doctorate in 1991.

Student life re-ignited an old passion, writing, and this has
continued ever since. David has composed over six hundred
poems, many short stories, and sketches, and eight extended
pieces. This collection of short stories spans some thirty-five
years, the first to be written, 'The Soul Train' dating from his
undergraduate years. He now lives in Edinburgh, where he
teaches and carries out research at Heriot-Watt University.